## PUFFIN BOOKS

### You're My Best Friend – I Hate You!

Rosie Rushton is a journalist with a particular interest in teenage and family relationship issues. She lives in Northamptonshire and has three grown-up daughters. Rosie Rushton has written five books for children and produced self-awareness work packs for use in schools. She is a regular contributor to Talk Radio UK, has written columns for regional and national newspapers and is freelance features editor of a regional magazine

*Other books by Rosie Rushton*


JUST DON'T MAKE A SCENE, MUM
STAYING COOL, SURVIVING SCHOOL

# YOU'RE MY BEST FRIEND –
# I HATE YOU!

## Friends – Getting, Losing and Keeping Them

**ROSIE RUSHTON**

*Illustrated by Kathryn Lamb*

PUFFIN BOOKS

PUFFIN BOOKS

Published by the Penguin Group
Penguin Books Ltd, 27 Wrights Lane, London W8 5TZ, England
Penguin Books USA Inc., 375 Hudson Street, New York, New York 10014, USA
Penguin Books Australia Ltd, Ringwood, Victoria, Australia
Penguin Books Canada Ltd, 10 Alcorn Avenue, Toronto, Ontario, Canada M4V 3B2
Penguin Books (NZ) Ltd, 182–190 Wairau Road, Auckland 10, New Zealand

Penguin Books Ltd, Registered Offices: Harmondsworth, Middlesex, England

First published by Piccadilly Press Ltd 1994
Published in Puffin Books 1996
1 3 5 7 9 10 8 6 4 2

Text copyright © Rosie Rushton, 1994
Illustrations copyright © Kathryn Lamb, 1994
All rights reserved

The moral right of the author has been asserted

Made and printed in Great Britain by Clays Ltd, St Ives plc

# CONTENTS

## 1. HELP! I NEED SOMEBODY     1-18
(Just How Important Are Friends?)

| | |
|---|---|
| WHERE IT ALL STARTS | 1 |
| WHAT MAKES SOMEONE A FRIEND? | 3 |
| WHAT MAKES A REAL FRIEND? | 5 |
| WHEN IS A FRIEND NOT A REAL FRIEND? | 6 |
| HOW IMPORTANT ARE YOU TO YOUR FRIENDS? | 7 |
| JUST HOW IMPORTANT ARE YOUR FRIENDS TO YOU? | 10 |
| TO BE GOOD FRIENDS, PEOPLE SOMETIMES HAVE TO ... | 16 |
| ALONE IS FINE – LONELY IS NOT | 16 |
| LIFE WITHOUT FRIENDS | 17 |

## 2. I LIKE ME, I LIKE YOU     19-49
(Gaining Confidence in the Friendship Stakes)

| | |
|---|---|
| RULES FOR FRIENDSHIP | 20 |
| Rule One: However Nice You Are, Not Everyone Is Going to Like You | 20 |
| Rule Two: To Get a Friend, You First Have to be Friends With Yourself | 22 |
| Rule Three: However Awful You May Think You Are, Someone Out There Will Think You Are Terrific | 23 |
| Rule Four: If You Really Like People, You Will Find Friends | 24 |
| Rule Five: Trying Too Hard is as Bad as Not Trying At All | 25 |

POPULARITY                                             26
  What Makes Someone Popular or Unpopular?        26
  When You're Unpopular and It's Not Your Fault    27
  Players in the Popular Pack                      28
  You Don't Have to be a "Star" to be a Friend     31
  How to Ensure that You Remain "One to Shun"      31
THE FOUR POINT PLAN TO MAKING FRIENDS                  32
  1. Learn to Communicate                          33
  2. Learn to Listen                               34
  3. Learn Not to Judge                            38
  4. Always be Yourself                            39
BOOSTING YOUR CONFIDENCE                               40
  Remedy One: How to Overcome Shyness              40
  Remedy Two: Who Says You Are Boring?             46
  Remedy Three: There's More to Life Than Tennis   47
  Remedy Four: Beauty is in the Eye of the Beholder  48

3.  GETTING FRIENDS, KEEPING FRIENDS  50-84
SIX SURE-FIRE WAYS TO FRIGHTEN AWAY POTENTIAL          51
  FRIENDS
SIX SURE-FIRE WAYS TO MAKE A NEW FRIEND WANT           52
  TO HANG AROUND
VARIETY IS THE SPICE OF LIFE                           55
GROUPS                                                 55
  What's So Great About Groups?                    56
  What's Not So Great About Groups?                59
  Are You a Good Groupy?                           59

BEST FRIENDS 62

What Makes a Friend into a Best Friend? 62

Have You Got What it Takes to be a Best Friend? 63

But Even Best Friends Have Their Moments 67

OTHER SORTS OF FRIENDS 69

The Once-in-à-while Friend 69

The Family Friend 71

Older Friends 73

Penfriends 73

Friends of the Opposite Sex 74

FORCED TO MAKE NEW FRIENDS: 79

PACK UP YOUR STUFF – WE'RE MOVING

What Your Parents Say and What You Say 80

Starting Over 82


4. POURING OIL ON TROUBLED WATERS 85-100

WHY DO FRIENDS FIGHT? 86

HOW DO THEY FIGHT? 86

WHAT SORTS OF SITUATION LEAD TO ROWS? 89

RULES FOR GETTING THE BEST OUT OF A ROW 90

HOW TO HANDLE A BUST-UP 94

WAYS OF SOLVING ARGUMENTS 96

FIVE FUN WAYS OF MAKING UP 97

ALL FRIENDS TOGETHER? 98

BEWARE THE GREEN-EYED MONSTER! 99

## 5. BUT IF I DON'T, THEY WON'T LIKE ME ANY MORE (Handling Peer Pressure)    101-121

YOUR PEERS AND PRESSURE    102

NO! – THE HARDEST WORD IN THE ENGLISH LANGUAGE    106

Why Do We Worry About Saying No?    107

How to Say No    109

People it's Very Hard to Say No to    110

WHEN THE RISKS JUST AREN'T WORTH THE HASSLE    113

When You're Doing Something Very Wrong    114

Smoking    115

Drinking    116

Drugs    118

SO HOW GOOD ARE YOU AT SAYING NO?    119

## 6. ME AND MY SHADOW    122-130

EVERYBODY'S DIFFERENT    123

Uniformly Splendid    123

Carrots, Celery and No-Cal Cola    126

FRIENDLY INFLUENCES    127

I Never Knew That    127

I Suppose They're Not All That Bad, Really    128

WHY DO YOU DO THAT?    130

## 7. MOVING ON – I REALLY LIKE YOU BUT ...    131-140

HOW TO HANDLE THE HANGERS-ON    133

WHEN THE BOOT IS ON THE OTHER FOOT  137
I CAN'T COME OUT WITH YOU – I'M IN LOVE  139

## 8. AND WHERE DID YOU FIND HIM?  141-150
(or What To Do When Your Parents Don't Adore
Your Friends)

WHY ARE PARENTS OFTEN CRITICAL OF  142
YOUR FRIENDS?
CHECKLIST FOR ENSURING THAT PARENTS GO ON  144
DISAPPROVING
CHECKLIST FOR PARENTS  146
WHEN PARENTS ARE WRONG  147
How to Get Your Parents on Your Side  147
FRIENDS FROM DIFFERENT CULTURES  149

## 9. I'D LIKE TO TEACH THE WORLD  151-160
TO SING ...

STRATEGIES FOR FRIENDLESS DAYS  152
1. Pamper Yourself  152
2. Stop Being So Hard on Yourself  153
3. Look Ahead  154
WHAT'S CRUCIAL NOW WON'T MATTER NEXT YEAR  155
THE PERFECT FRIEND – YOU!  159

## Chapter 1

# HELP! I NEED SOMEBODY
### (Just How Important Are Friends?)

*"A friend is one who comes in when the whole world has gone out."*
**(Alban Goodier)**

## WHERE IT ALL STARTS

When you were a new-born baby, the only thing that really mattered to you was getting enough to eat, being given somewhere warm and comfortable to sleep and having Mum or Dad cuddle you when the nappy pin stuck in somewhere nasty or you threw up all your pureed apricot over Teddy's blue bow tie.

But after a few months, when you were pretty good at recognising Mum and Dad but not quite so good at getting them to understand what you were trying to say, you got bored and started looking around for someone else to take an interest in. There was Grandma who peered into your buggy and made silly noises at you, and Granddad who threw you up in the air and made you yell – but they were all much bigger than you, could move very fast without falling over, talked gibberish and put you to bed when you weren't tired. What you were looking for was someone JUST LIKE YOU.

And then it happened. One day in the park, in between beating the living daylights out of your fluffy panda and trying to make your mouth say "I am starving hungry and would like a large vanilla cone, please," you saw it.

Another Small Person.

Just like you.

You tried a tentative gurgle.

It gurgled back.

You leaned out of your buggy and aimed a fairly untrained left hook at its rubber duck.

It grinned at you.

You smiled back.

You'd done it! You had made the first, shaky steps towards Finding a Friend.

But then you made another important discovery.

2

*The Friendship Business isn't quite as easy as it looks.*

After a few meetings in the park, having a quick rattle bash or pulling each other's socks off, the Mother People decided that this was A Good Thing. Suddenly this other Small Person was coming back to *your* house, being plonked down on *your* rug and even being offered a rusk out of *your* packet.

This was not how you had planned it.

So rather than let the situation get out of hand, you snatched back the rusk, gave a deft kick with your bootee-clad left foot, which sent the intruder flying off the rug and then yelled as loudly as your lungs would allow, just to ensure that no-one was left in any doubt about your feelings on the matter.

And then a most surprising thing happened. Your mother picked you up and told you not to be "a naughty little girl" or "such a horrid little boy" and to "be nice to your little friend". Friend? you thought. What's this new word? What's a Friend?

## WHAT MAKES SOMEONE A FRIEND?

When you are a baby, a friend is:
• Someone who teaches you how to blow raspberries and then laughs when you get told off.
• Someone who doesn't turn a hair if you fall asleep in the middle of the Rosie and Jim video, or throw your creamed rice in the fireplace.
• Someone who can teach you how to suck your big toe

3

and make one pot of raspberry yoghurt cover an entire three-piece suite.

But even at that age, you discover that a friend is also:
• Someone you have to share your Fisher Price airport with, even if they want the helicopter all the time.
• Someone who turns up to stay the night even when you are not in the mood for sharing your bedroom.
• Someone who is allowed to eat their pudding before they've finished their fish finger.
• Someone who gives you a great big hug – and the chickenpox.
  But the best discovery of all is that a friend is:
• Someone who, even after you've pinched their pullalong dog and eaten their last chocolate button, still likes you almost as much as their teddy bear.

So by the time you are ready for playgroup you have learned three important things about friendship:
1. It's all about give and take.
2. It's a lot more fun than being stuck on your own with a kangaroo mobile and a box of building bricks.
3. It's quite a bit harder than getting your thumb into your mouth first time or spitting creamed banana dessert at the cat.

But as you grow older, things get even more complicated. You discover that before you can distinguish between People You Know and Real Friends, you have to hit some bad times. Any old relationship can jog along when everything goes swimmingly, but only Real Friends hang around when the going gets tough.

## WHAT MAKES A REAL FRIEND?

A Real Friend is someone who:
• Is just as happy to spend time helping you with your history project and eating popcorn as she is to go shopping or party the night away.
• Turns out in the freezing cold to act as goalie while you practise your kicks – because he knows how much being selected for the school football team means to you.
• Knows that you still take a scrawny rabbit to bed with you and that you are scared of earwigs – and doesn't tell a soul.
• Misses two meals and the Test Match on television to help you mend your bike.
• Lets you cry on her shoulder when the boy you fancy goes off with Melanie from next door – and doesn't moan if your so-called waterproof mascara ends up on her collar.
• Lends you her silk shirt the evening you get invited out by that cool kid from Year Ten.
• Lends you her hanky when the cool kid doesn't phone.
• Tells his sister that you are one cool guy because he knows you want her to go to the disco with you on Saturday night.
• Has the courage to tell you if she thinks you are about to make a complete idiot of yourself – and understands if

you don't take a blind bit of notice!
• Doesn't yell at you when you have to watch Grandstand because you forgot to get tickets for the local Derby.
• Doesn't mind if you call her up in the middle of *The Bill* because your boyfriend has just been seen in the arcade with that willowy blonde, Samantha Clegthorpe, and you think your life is over.
• Is there for you, no matter what.

Of course, there are times when a new friendship starts out really well and looks like it's going to last forever – and then something happens to make you realise that it's not quite what it seemed.

## WHEN IS A FRIEND NOT A REAL FRIEND?

• When they tell you that you look terrific in your grunge-look outfit, knowing full well you resemble a bin bag that's been left out in the rain – because they want to be the best-looking kid around.
• When they listen to you unburdening your soul to them – and then rush off and tell all your secrets to the first five people they meet.
• When they criticise all your other friends and threaten to stop speaking to you if you don't ditch the lot of them – remember, they are probably running you down as soon as your back is turned.
• When the only time they come to see you is when they want to borrow your French prep/curling tongs/

Eurhythmics CD.
• When they arrange to go to the cinema with you and then call up to cancel because a better offer turned up.

For a friendship to really work, you both need to be really important to each other.

## HOW IMPORTANT ARE YOU TO YOUR FRIENDS?

1. You are stuck in bed with chickenpox, feeling spotty and itchy and unloved. You call up your friend Louise and burst into tears. Does she:
(a) Come round with a pile of magazines, a Body Shop soothing gel and all the latest gossip?
(b) Say "Jolly bad luck" and promise to visit when the spots have gone?
(c) Tell you she can't talk now because *Home and Away* is on TV?

2. You are having a really hard time understanding a physics project and your friend Chris is a real whiz at all things scientific. Does he:
(a) Offer to sit down and give you some ideas about getting started?
(b) Lend you his notes, saying "It's ever so easy, anyone can do it"?
(c) Laugh, say "Oh Phil, you are so utterly thick," and

proceed to tell the entire class that you don't understand hydraulics?

3. Your mum and dad are going through a bad patch and there's a lot of arguing at home. You need someone to talk to – and talk and talk and talk. You turn to your friend Emily. Does she:
(a) Yawn, look bored, and say "Yes, I know, you've told me three times already"?
(b) Say "Well, if it's so tough at home, come to my house because *my* parents love each other."
(c) Listen, listen and listen some more and then take you out for a Coke and a doughnut to cheer you up?

4. You are having a hard time at school being bullied by Big Ego in the Year Nine. You tell your friend Mandy that you can't stand it much longer. Does she:
(a) Say "Oh, grow up and don't be such a jerk"?
(b) Say "Just do what he says and he'll leave you alone"?
(c) Go straight to your form teacher with you, or to the Head, or her mum and tell them the whole story?

*NOW CHECK THEM OUT*:
1. (a) 5 points. This is true friendship. It is a well known medical fact that gossip, glamour mags and a grin can kill most bugs at ten paces.
    (b) 3. At least she is sympathetic and it may be that her mum is neurotic about germs and doesn't want the other kids and the gerbils coming out in spots. But *did* she turn up after your spots had gone?

(c) 0. Anyone who puts a soap before a friend in need isn't worth bothering about.

2. (a) 5. True friends offer a helping hand. Doing the whole project for you wouldn't have helped come exam time when you still didn't understand the question. But pointing the way makes all the difference.

(b) 2. He's generous with his notes but they probably make as much sense to you as an Arabic newspaper and ten minutes of his time would have been more valuable.

(c) 0. True friends don't make fun of other people's weak points.

3. (a) 0. Low on compassion, this one. Family traumas are more upsetting than anything else you go through but this friend doesn't care enough to be any help. One day it might happen to her.

(b) 3. She probably means to be kind but she doesn't realise that she is just rubbing in the fact that everything is hunky-dory in her world while yours is (you think) falling apart.

(c) 5. A gem. Not only does she give you her care and her time but she fills you up with carbohydrate which is just what you need when you are feeling mizz. She will go far.

4. (a) 0. She simply doesn't care.

(b) 0. Sounds like the easy way out, doesn't it? Except that Bully will ask for more and more and your life will get more and more miserable. What this friend means is

Count Me Out.

(c) 5. True friendship. This course of action takes guts but it's the only way to deal with what could become a very dangerous situation. Remember to stand by this friend come what may. She might need your support one day.

*SO HOW DID THEY FARE?*

0–5. Oh dear. This "friend" would be better consigned to the "someone I once knew and thought I liked" pile.
6–10. They mean well but don't always get it right. Nurture them and be patient. They'll learn.
11–16. A pretty good sort and someone who can be relied on to turn up trumps most of the time.
17 and over: Cherish this friend – they don't come much better.

And now let's put the boot on the other foot!

# JUST HOW IMPORTANT ARE YOUR FRIENDS TO YOU?

1. You've been invited to a party in your old home town and you take your friend Jenny with you. She doesn't know anyone there. Do you:
(a) Introduce her to lots of people as soon as you arrive, telling them all what a great friend she is?
(b) Talk to her for a couple of minutes and then drift off to chat to old mates, leaving her clutching a cold sausage

and feeling like a lemon?
(c) Shove a glass of Coca Cola in her hands and say "See ya on the last bus"?

2. Your friend Sam broke his leg playing rugby and the doctors say he cannot play for the rest of the season. He is really cut up about it and rings you for a moan. Do you:
(a) Say "For heaven's sake, it's only a stupid game."
(b) Say "Well, you were never exactly Will Carling, were you?"
(c) Tell him that some of the best rugby internationals have had seasons off and that his game will be even better when he returns – and then persuade your dad to lend him his videos of the Calcutta Cup?

3. Your friend Liz has fancied a boy for weeks and at last he has asked her out. She begs you to go shopping with her to help her choose something to wear. Do you:
(a) Go along reluctantly and spend all the time searching for some new eyeliner, saying you are bored and telling her that purple makes her look fat?
(b) Say you can't see what she sees in him and anyway, you're waxing your legs that day?
(c) Follow her from shop to shop, telling her honestly what looks good on her and offering to lend her your favourite Indian bead necklace?

4. Your friend Mark confides in you that he really fancies your sister's best friend, Emily. He wants to ask her out but feels too shy. Do you:

(a) Roar with laughter and shout to all your other mates, "Hey, guess what, dimbo Mark here fancies. Emily – is he mad or what?"
(b) Sigh, say, "Oh well, if you are into girls, I'm off," and refuse to have anything to do with him for the rest of the week?
(c) Find out when your sister is having Emily over to your house and make sure you invite Mark to be around at the same time?

5. Your friend Mia has had a big bust-up with her other friend Lisa. Both Mia and Lisa come to you separately, moaning about the other one – and confessing that they wish they could be friends again. Do you:
(a) Tell Mia that it was all Lisa's fault and she's a glob, and then tell Lisa it was Mia's fault because she's a nutcase?
(b) Feel pleased that they've fallen out because now they will both spend more time with you – and tell them both that they are well rid of each other?
(c) Invite them both round to your house, pour out the coffee and then remember an urgent phone call, leaving them to make up on neutral ground?

6. You are having one of those globby days when you feel angry with the world at large and are sure nothing will ever go right again. Your best friend asks you what is wrong. Do you:
(a) Say "Mind your own stupid business," turn your back and flounce out of the room?

(b) Say "You are – you've been getting on my nerves for days"?

(c) Say "I don't know – I just feel fed up and miserable"?

7. You lend your friend Marcus your favourite Beverley Craven tape and he gets it all mangled up in his dad's car tape deck. He apologises and says he will replace it but you are pretty certain it is no longer available. Do you:

(a) Say "OK, thanks – car tape decks are so unreliable, aren't they?"

(b) Say "Well, that's marvellous, that is – it was my favourite and anyway you won't find another one and why did you have to be such a complete geek?"

(c) Refuse to lend him anything ever again and then tell everyone in the class what happened?

## HOW DO YOU RATE AS A MATE?

1. (a) 5. Spot on. Boosting your friend's image will make her feel good and make other people want to get to know her better.

   (b) 2. Never leave a friend alone at a party – wait till she is chatting to someone before you move on.

   (c) 0. What did you take her for? Company on the bus?

2. (a) 2. What you probably mean is "Don't upset yourself," but these sporty types go puce in the face if you call their fix "just a game". To them it ranks as high in importance as breathing.

   (b) 0. The poor chap is feeling bad enough as it is; don't make matters even worse.

(c) 5. Great. You probably haven't a clue about the effect of injury on future play, but it will cheer him up and the videos were a stroke of genius.

3. (a) 0. You are supposed to be helping her, not thinking of yourself and making snide remarks.
   (b) 0. What's a hairy leg compared to a friend?
   (c) 5. She'll do the same for you one day.

4. (a) 0. Jeering at someone else's feelings is pretty low – and the only dimbo on the scene is you.
   (b) 2. At least you are getting out of his way instead of making fun of him – but that is not friendship. Could it be that you are jealous?
   (c) 5. Great idea. That way Mark and Emily get to find out whether they do really like one another and you are proving that you are there to support him whatever happens.

5. (a) 0. How do you know whose fault it was – and how can you call yourself a friend if all you do is say mean things about other people?
   (b) 0. Actually, it's you they would be well rid of.
   (c) 5. Brilliant. Just make sure you spend long enough with that "phone call" to get them talking and not long enough for them to have another row!

6. (a) 1. The only benefit of this is that it gets you and your black mood out of your friend's way – she was only trying to help.

(b) 0. Never accuse other people of being the source of your miseries unless they really are.

(c) 5. There is nothing to be ashamed of in admitting that you feel grotty and don't know why. Everyone has days like that – try a large chocolate bar, a hot bath with lavender oil in it and a moan to your friend.

7. (a) 5. You are putting the blame on the machine, not on your friend, who is probably feeling rotten enough anyway. And by agreeing to let him try to replace it, he feels he is doing something positive to make amends.

(b) 0. There is no point going on and on about something that has already happened and can't be altered. You are just making him feel small and getting yourself into a state.

(c) 1. He had an accident – why hold it against him? Have you never broken, lost or damaged anything belonging to someone else?

*HOW DO YOU MEASURE UP ON THE CHUM CHART?*
0–6: Perhaps you had better think it through again.
7–15: Remember that putting people down, criticising their every move and poking fun at their weaknesses isn't clever – it's plain mean. And in the end the only person to look stupid is you.
16–19: Just because someone sees things differently from you, or gets upset by things that wouldn't bother you, does not mean their feelings matter less. With a bit more thought about how it feels to be on the other end, you could make yourself sound a lot friendlier.

20–25: You're getting there – just mellow out a little more.
26–32: Nice, aren't you?
33–35: Are you sure you didn't cheat?

## TO BE GOOD FRIENDS, PEOPLE SOMETIMES HAVE TO ...

• Forego doing something they want to do in order to be there when their friend has a tooth pulled out/tells their mum they've lost their blazer/tells their boyfriend he's a jerk.
• Swallow their pride and admit they were wrong to borrow their friend's maths book without asking/tell tales behind their back/call them a dimbo.
• Understand that their friends have the right to spend time with other people and not sulk when they don't get invited to everything that's going on.
• Listen to their problems – and not be offended when they fail to act on your advice.

## ALONE IS FINE – LONELY IS NOT

Of course, you may say, "I don't need friends – I like my own company."

Just remember, being alone sometimes is fine – but being lonely is pretty grim. There is nothing wrong in enjoying your own company – in fact it is a good thing to be able to be content without constantly needing other people around you. Quiet times are important for thinking your own thoughts, curling up with a good book, cutting your toenails and doing nothing.

But being alone too much has its drawbacks. If you have had a bad day, brooding on it makes it worse, and if you've had a mega-magnificent day, it is good to have someone to share it with. After all, if you were alone all the time, who would you share that Double Bonanza Triple-Topped Multi-Spiced Pizza with?

But it's worth it. Just think what life would be like without friends.

## LIFE WITHOUT FRIENDS

• You would have to wear your own clothes all the time and never get the chance to find out whether Miranda's cerise silk camisole or Tammy's paisley waistcoat suited you.
• When you made that vow never to speak to your family ever again, you would be left talking to the budgie and the rubber plant.
• Who would help you do your roots?
• Who would help you find the right way home when you got lost orienteering?
• Who would you tell about your passion for Simon Snodgrass in Year Ten?
• Who would you tell when you discovered that Simon was a nerd?

17

• Who would you cling to on the Nemesis ride at Alton Towers?

• Who would let you in on the secret of how to get Sonic the Hedgehog to capture the extra 100 points on top of the viaduct?

• Who would you talk to half the night on the telephone while baby-sitting your little brother?

• Who would share all your triumphs, disasters, raspberry milk shakes and detentions?

In short, if we didn't have friends, growing up would be a pretty miserable process and being grown up would be intolerable.

## Chapter 2

# I LIKE ME, I LIKE YOU

(Gaining confidence in the friendship stakes)

*"One does not make friends, one recognises them."*
Isabel Paterson

All of us want to be liked. The good news is that nearly all of us are pretty likeable people. True, we all have our not-so-charming sides – like leaving decaying apple cores under the bed or picking our noses in Human Biology –

but when the chips are down we are the sort who would share our last Rolos, cover up for Bella Bassenthwaite by saying she's in the loo when really she's chatting up Kevin Keene behind the CDT block, and even let our sister use our best lipstick before her big night out. In short, we're pretty terrific people. So why doesn't everyone adore us?

## RULES FOR FRIENDSHIP

### RULE ONE: HOWEVER NICE YOU ARE, NOT EVERYONE IS GOING TO LIKE YOU

Little kids want – and expect – the entire universe to love them, but because human beings are all so different, it simply can't work that way. Look at these examples.

1. Diana is 13, mad on horses and her dog Max, and not very keen on school. Her parents both work full-time, her two older brothers have left home and she spends most of her spare time riding or helping out at the local stables. She is friendly and has a good sense of humour but still gets on better with animals than people.

   Diana's idea of the perfect friend: "Someone who loves riding and prefers being outdoors to inside. I'm not very keen on parties and clothes. I'd like a friend who preferred doing things rather than sitting around and chatting."

2. Tony is 11 and a computer whizz kid. He writes his own

computer games and won the school computer studies prize last year. He loves puzzles of all sorts but hates sport. He spends a lot of time with his younger brother Russ, who is ten, and when he is not at his computer, he likes playing the drums and listening to pop music.

Tony's idea of the perfect friend: "I don't mean to sound big-headed or anything, but I'd like a friend who was better than me at computer games. Lots of my friends from school come round to my house to play on the computer but because I win most of the time, they get fed up and so do I. And it would be fun to have someone to set up a band with – just for a laugh."

3. Kim is 14, loves sport, especially tennis, and is not very good at academic subjects. Her dad died three years ago and most of her spare time is spent helping her Mum look after her three younger sisters, aged ten, seven and six. She would like to be a PE teacher when she leaves school. She doesn't have much pocket money and can't afford to go out often. She is very friendly but shy with strangers.

Kim's idea of a perfect friend: "Someone like my best friend Emily who moved to Australia last year. I really miss her. Most of my friends don't understand why I can't go out whenever they phone up but if my Mum is working, I have to keep an eye on the other kids. I'd like someone to play tennis with down the park at weekends but I don't want a rich friend because you always end up feeling the odd one out."

Three very likeable people. Three very normal people.

Three people with very different tastes in friends.

## RULE TWO: TO GET A FRIEND, YOU FIRST HAVE TO BE FRIENDS WITH YOURSELF

Sounds daft? Think about it. If you believe that you are stupid, ugly or boring, then you will sit around looking glum and feeling miserable and all those little vibes that you send out to other people will say, "Hey guys, I'm a pretty dull person actually – I can't imagine why you should want to be friends with me."

When you are feeling down, you probably tell yourself:

"If I lose half a stone, everyone will like me."

"If only I could afford those Reeboks and an acid perm, Mark would think I was great."

"If my parents would let me stay out later at night, I could get in with the right crowd."

"If we lived in a big house, I'd have lots of friends." Imagining that the world would flock to your side if you had a designer lifestyle or plenty of cash is frankly rubbish. Let's think again. What if you lost that half stone? Would it make you kinder? Wittier? Would, in fact, anyone notice? Would anyone care? If you had those Reeboks and the curly hair, and if Mark did notice, would he hang around because he thought, "Gee, this girl is great – just look at those trainers and I love the smell of perm lotion"? Of course not. And if your mum and dad suddenly threw away the clock and the rule book and let you stay out till all hours, would the gang take you to

22

their hearts? They might – for a week or so. But the only thing that would keep you there would be your personality, your sense of fun – in short, your worth as a friend. As for the big house, why should that make any difference? If you are not friendly and fun to be with, you could live in Buckingham Palace and no-one would come to call. So why not try listing all the good things about you that make you a great person to be someone's friend? Your house may not be huge, but if it is a welcoming place to be, your friends will flock there. If you are the sort of person who likes a laugh and a joke, you are worth a dozen glamour pusses. And if you don't mind helping out when your friends are in a fix, you will find yourself at the centre of all that is going on. Maybe you are good with your hands, brilliant at fixing things and just the guy to design the club go-kart for the Children in Need Sponsored Dash. Everyone has good points and everyone has bad ones. The trick is to emphasise the first and try to blot out the second.

## RULE THREE: HOWEVER AWFUL YOU MAY THINK YOU ARE, SOMEONE OUT THERE WILL THINK YOU ARE TERRIFIC

You wake up in the morning, look at yourself in the mirror and promptly wish you hadn't. You are convinced that your hair is hideous, your stomach sagging and you've just seen two spots sprouting on your neck. What's more, yesterday you came bottom in French, let two goals in during hockey, much to the disgust of your team, and had a blazing row with Katrina because she spilt your new nail polish in the sink. In short, you are convinced that your friends and the world at large hate you. Good. This proves *you are just the same as about ten million other kids.*

Let's just look at what you think you would like to be *The Greatest Girl That Ever Lived:*
1. Top in everything from history to home economics.
2. The best sportswoman the school has ever seen.
3. Totally stunning, with flowing chestnut tresses, a flawless skin and a perfect figure.
4. Utterly loveable, always in a good mood, never bossy or argumentative, and never ever given to throwing your geography folder at the cat.

You think everyone would love you? No way.

Why? Because everyone is human and no-one likes to have perfection rammed down their throats. If you were that perfect, you might attract a few friends for a week or even a month. But they would soon get tired of your unfailing brilliance and start looking for someone with a few human failings.


## RULE FOUR: IF YOU REALLY LIKE PEOPLE, YOU WILL FIND FRIENDS

Of course, there will be plenty of people you meet and don't particularly like. But are you interested in what makes other people tick? Do you want to find out why

Dougie is so smitten with stock-car racing while Jemma thinks modern jazz is the only kind of music worth listening to? Are you keen to find out more about how Rajiv's family celebrate Diwali or why Ismail doesn't eat school lunch during Ramadan? Or are you of the mind that your way is the only way and it's up to the others to fit in with you?

## RULE FIVE: TRYING TOO HARD IS AS BAD AS NOT TRYING AT ALL

Have you ever sat on the school bus and watched Penny Popular holding court on the back seat, telling everyone about the party she is going to have – and just known that you won't be getting an invitation? Or stood in a group of kids at the start of football, with that awful sinking feeling in the pit of your stomach, sure that you will be the one that's left at the end of the team-picking session?

So you start desperately trying to be like the Popular People. You copy their hairstyles, imitate the way they dress, try to muscle in on their conversations and even pretend you like the things they like, just to get included. But is this really the way to go about it? After all, it can be pretty exhausting pretending to be someone you are not all the time. It's much easier to be yourself. All you need to do is ask your ageing granny about the words of a very old song that she used to sing in the days before she went tone deaf: "*Accentuate the positive, eliminate the negative.*" Or to put it more simply, make a big deal out of your good points and try to wipe out, or at least trample on, the less appealing aspects.

# POPULARITY

FACT: *Everyone wants to be popular.*

To be "in" makes you feel that you are someone who matters – to be "out" makes you feel like a nothing. But don't decide that you simply *have* to be best friends with the most popular person or that life will end if you are not part of the current "in" crowd. If they obviously don't like you, look elsewhere – you will find plenty of people who do. And remember – this term's "in" gang could be next term's outcasts. Real friendship goes beyond joining up with people just because they are the centre of attention today.

That is not to say that there are not pointers to popularity. Many people are popular simply because they are Nice Guys. So who are the ones who make up the Popular Pack? And how do you get to join them?

## WHAT MAKES SOMEONE POPULAR OR UNPOPULAR?

POPULAR
1. Being friendly

UNPOPULAR
1. Being stand-offish – though you might give this impression simply because you feel shy

2. Being helpful
3. Being good-natured
4. Having a sense of humour
5. Being confident
6. Being responsive
7. Being enthusiastic
   and fun and taking part

2. Being arrogant
3. Being aggressive
4. Being a killjoy
5. Being a tell-tale
6. Being self-centred
7. Never contributing or
   having ideas of your own

Look around at those of your mates who are really popular and you will find that they have at least three of the attributes in the first column, while the guys no-one really wants around (the ones who miss out on party invitations, get left out of secrets and don't get many Christmas cards) probably display at least two of the not-so-jolly characteristics of the second column.

But there are other reasons why people are unpopular.

## WHEN YOU'RE UNPOPULAR AND IT'S NOT YOUR FAULT

Perhaps the most popular person in the class has taken against you and everyone is following their lead; perhaps the school bully has picked on you – and everyone is scared that if they befriend you, they will be the next target. If you feel you are unpopular, make an *honest* list of the reasons why you think you might be.

It could be because:
1. You are a different colour/creed/race – people are often bigoted and frightened of anything they don't

properly understand.

2. You are always top of the class – sometimes people feel jealous and put down by highly successful friends, especially if those friends boast and brag about their achievements.

3. You are never prepared to pull your weight and take your turn at things – everyone has to have a go at the boring jobs sometimes.

4. You are very shy, and you give the wrong impression – people think you're stand-offish and arrogant.


## PLAYERS IN THE POPULAR PACK

*CHEERFUL CHERYL AND CHORTLING CHARLIE*
*How to spot them:* Always grinning and seeing the funny side of life. Unfazed even on those days when it's pouring with rain, the Lisa Stansfield concert is sold out and River Island are fresh out of crushed velvet leggings.

*Why are they popular?* We all need to be cheered on our way and these types are brilliant at making even the blackest day seem brighter. They rarely seem to worry about little things, and people like to be with them because they make them feel that maybe there is a light at the end of the tunnel and one day they might understand past participles, stop rowing with their mum and get the better of their acne.

*How can you be like them?* Remember that people are more likely to want to be with you if you smile rather than sulk or are ready with a joke rather than a jibe.

### INSPIRED ISABEL AND INGENIOUS IAN
*How to spot them:* These are the Great Ideas Guys. Never at a loss for a good excuse in an emergency/a quick way of getting through detention/bright ideas for persuading parents to fork out for a Sleepover Party.

*Why are they so popular?* Because unlike some people, they are perfectly happy to share their brilliant scams with everyone else. If they have discovered a way to write 1000 lines in 10 minutes flat, they will tell anyone who asks. Need a plan for persuading Dad to lend you a fiver? Isabel and Ian will have it wrapped up by teatime.

*How can you be like them?* You may not be hot on ideas but you will be surprised at how clever you can be when you are part of a team. Start offering to help out in any schemes that there are, and join in the discussions on how to raise money for the school ski trip to Switzerland.

### KEEN KAREN AND ENTHUSIASTIC EDDIE
*How to spot them:* Willing to do anything from starting a basketball club to bathing in baked beans for Children in Need.

*Why are they popular?* Because they enter heart and soul into whatever is going on and never think for one moment that it might not work out. They don't mind making idiots of themselves for a laugh and their enthusiasm is so infectious that it makes other people want to join in.

*How can you be like them?* Stop thinking up excuses why *not* to join in, and give it a whirl. OK, so you might feel a bit silly or self-conscious to begin with but you will soon be having too much fun to care what you look like.

## CARING CASSIE AND COMPASSIONATE CHRIS

*How to spot them:* Usually have damp patches on their shirts where friends have sobbed on their shoulders. Great for helping hedgehogs and old ladies to cross roads and brilliant as stand-in agony aunts and uncles. Often short of cash because they have lent it to Sarah who forgot her dinner money or John for his bus fare. Usually accompanied by a bird with a broken wing/pregnant endangered toad/collecting box for the homeless.

*Why are they popular?* People who genuinely care about others are never short of friends. Deep down, we all want to be loved, cherished and cheered and we all worry that one day we will be the ones needing someone to lean on.

*How can you be like them?* Be there to lend an ear when your friends need you – even if you were just about to go shopping or nip out for a Big Mac. Sometimes it is harder than it sounds: if a friend's mum is very ill or their granddad has just died, we tend to think that because we don't know what to say, we will be of no use. But at times like this, what most people need is a friendly ear. And you have two of those.

## YOU DON'T HAVE TO BE A "STAR" TO BE A FRIEND

There will always be those who are popular because they are stunning to look at, clever at everything from algebra to ancient history, or the sort of people who never seem scared of anything. Everyone might want to be friends with Neil Knott because his dad is roadie for the biggest group in pop history and they all want tickets to the next gig – but they might not really like him as a person. Miranda might suddenly be flavour of the month when she announces that her parents have just finished installing a heated swimming pool in their back garden – but it could be that it is the poolside barbecues they are interested in rather than Miranda herself. Real popularity means you are well-liked because of *you*, not because of what you can get for your friends.

It's great to be popular in the sense that people flock to your side in droves, but real friendship is even better. It is far more important to have two people you can count on through thick and thin than a whole host of hangers-on who are only there for what they can get out of you now.

## HOW TO ENSURE THAT YOU REMAIN "ONE TO SHUN"

1. Be like Aggressive Andrew – snap people's heads off when they don't agree with your point of view, shove your way to the front of every queue, and snarl at anyone who steals the limelight from your wonderful self.

2. Copy Self-centred Simon – talk only about what you can do, what you want to be and where you went last night. Agree only to schemes in which you can have the leading role, the last word and the only point of view.

3. Imitate Killjoy Kimberly and greet every suggestion with "Well, it can't possibly work out" or "You'll never do it" or "It's bound to rain anyway."

4. Turn your nose up like Snobbish Sebastian and Snooty Sinead. Begin sentences with "Oh, in *my* family we don't do it that way!" or "Golly, have you only got one car?"

5. And if you really want to be left out on your own, why not be like Telltale Trudi and Sneaky Shaun? Never keep a secret, always drop other people in it and never, ever turn a blind eye to your friend's faults and failings.

## THE FOUR POINT PLAN TO MAKING FRIENDS

Some people can make friends really quickly. A quick "Hi, I'm Julie" and a shared Coke and it is as if they had known one another for years. Other people take much longer, feeling their way and taking time to relax enough to build up confidences. That's because people have different personalities – some are outgoing, carefree and uninhibited, others are more reserved, shy and cautious. But with a bit of thought, even the shyest person can find making friends a lot easier than they imagine.

You wouldn't expect to leave school and get a job before you had mastered the art of reading, writing and counting. Everyone knows you need those skills before you can earn your own living. In the same way, you need to learn how to be a good friend and a well-liked person. Remember when you were a baby in the park? You had to learn that hitting people with your rattle or throwing their mittens into the mud was not the best way to make friends (well, not with their mothers, anyway). At playgroup you learned to share your paints and take it in turns to play in the sandbox, and at school you learned that you cannot always be team leader, school prefect or leading lady in the Christmas panto. And the lessons go on and on.

## 1. LEARN TO COMMUNICATE
*"The language of friendship is not words, but meanings."*
Henry Thoreau

Sounds easy, doesn't it? We are pretty good at talking, especially when the subject is *us*. It is by talking with friends that we discover the things we have in common and the things on which we just don't see eye to eye. But sometimes we are bad at getting our message across.

*What we say*: Go away and leave me alone.
*What we mean*: I'm about to burst into tears and I'll feel an idiot if you see me cry.
*A better way of putting it*: I'm not in a very happy mood

right now – how about we talk after school?

*What we say*: You look awful – like death warmed up.
*What we mean*: You look awful – is it the lime green
leotard or that new henna rinse?
*A better way of putting it*: You look rather pale – are you
sure you are feeling OK?

*What we say*: I look a real mess, don't I?
*What we mean*: Please say I look terrific or I won't dare set
foot outside the house.
*A better way of putting it*: I'm not sure that I've got this
outfit quite right – what do you reckon?

*What we say*: Er – hi, Sandy – must dash – got a piano
lesson.
*What we mean*: Sandy, I just don't know how to talk to
you about your dad getting killed in that car accident so I
am running off rather than risk saying the wrong thing.
*A better way of putting it*: I just don't know what to say
about your dad – but if you ever want to talk, you know
you can come to me any time.


## 2. LEARN TO LISTEN

And that doesn't just mean hearing what people are
saying, but understanding what they are not saying as
well. There is nothing worse if you are feeling at a low ebb
and want to have a jolly good moan about love, life and

your mother's terrible dress sense, than to have someone interrupt and say "Oh, I know, and did I tell you about ..."

Listening sounds as easy as talking, doesn't it? I mean, all you do is sit there, picking the nail varnish off your thumb and murmuring "Ooh I say" and "Never" and occasionally "I told you so." Isn't it? No, it isn't.

## YOU DON'T JUST LISTEN WITH YOUR EARS, YOU LISTEN WITH YOUR EYES AND YOUR BODY

For one thing, when you are at a loss for words, an understanding glance or sympathetic smile can speak volumes. And for another, if you are not watching your friend while she talks, you miss all those little gestures and body expressions that tell you as much about how she is feeling as the actual words she speaks. If you turn your body away from her, just as she starts to tell you why she is worried sick about her dad, you give the impression that you are shutting her out; fiddling with your shoelace or rearranging your hair while Dave is trying to explain why he fell out with his best mate suggests that you put your beauty before his problem.

Quite often people don't really say what they mean. Look at these examples:

*What your friend says:* Do you think this is a boil coming up on my neck?
*What she means:* I'm scared I've got cancer because lumps mean cancer, don't they?
*What your friend says:* Doesn't Bill sound stupid now his voice is beginning to break?

*What he means:* I am really bothered because mine hasn't started changing yet. Do you think there is something wrong with me?

*What your friend says:* My mum is going to marry that awful Nigel – how could she?
*What she means:* Since my dad left, it's been just Mum and me and now I am scared that she won't want me anymore because she'll have him.

Sometimes friends pluck up the courage to talk about really important things – and the other person just won't let them speak.

*Sue:* How are your mum and dad getting on these days?
*Zoe:* Well, not too badly, but the real problem is my gran because ...
*Sue:* Oh, don't talk to me about grandmothers – mine is a real tartar. Do you know, the other day ...
*Zoe:* Oh no, it's nothing like that. My gran is really lovely; it's just that ...
*Sue:* Well, you're lucky, that's all I can say. Mine is always going on about my hair and my table manners and ...
*Zoe:* No, you see, my gran has ...
*Sue:* And the other day, my gran told my mum that I talked too much. What do you think of that?

Sue never got to hear that Zoe's gran had broken her hip and Zoe's mum wanted her to come and live with them.

Zoe would have to give up her bedroom and she felt all mixed up about it. The problem with Sue was that she had never learned to listen.

*WHILE YOU LISTEN, DON'T RIDICULE*
Avoid saying things like "Oh come on, Lucy, it's not that tragic ... " or "Oh for pity's sake, pull yourself together." If a friend has taken the plunge and entrusted their confidences to you, at least show them the courtesy of listening until they have finished.

*TRY NOT TO KEEP GIVING ADVICE – UNTIL IT'S ASKED FOR*
If your friend is in full flood about how unfair her parents are being about not letting her have a party, don't begin, "Now this is what you have to do" until you have heard the full story – and until she says, "What do you think I should do?" While she is talking, she may be working out a perfectly sensible answer in her own head – talking does that sometimes.

*NEVER TREAT YOUR FRIENDS' PROBLEMS TOO LIGHTLY*
You may think Amelia's worries over whether to paint her bedroom ceiling black or yellow are trivial – but if she's paying for the paint and expecting a rollicking from her dad if it looks awful, she won't thank you for saying, "Oh, is that all?" and wandering off to the sweet machine.

## 3. LEARN NOT TO JUDGE

We all have days when we think our friends have gone totally mad or are behaving in a stupid fashion. We have times when we think they are deliberately trying to make us mad and days when it seems that whatever we want to do, they are determined to do the opposite. But very often, there is a sound reason for their behaviour.

"My friend Sally always came out on Saturdays – either to the cinema or the roller rink. Suddenly she said it was boring and childish and stopped coming. I asked her if she wanted to do something else but she told me to get lost. So I told her she was boring anyway, and that was that." (Maria, aged 13)

   *What really happened:* "I discovered two weeks later that Sally's dad had lost his job and so she didn't get an allowance any more. And her mum wanted her to stay in with her baby sister on Saturdays so that she could go out to work to earn more money. I felt really rotten when I found out the truth."

"When I started my new school, I made friends with this really nice guy called Sandeep. We both like playing tennis and we entered the school mixed doubles and everything. One day, I called at his flat above the Tandoori takeaway where his dad is manager. The next day, Sandeep was really off with me and said he was scratching from the tournament because he had too much school work. I couldn't understand why and I called him all sorts of names – some of them pretty racist, I am ashamed to say." (Glynis, aged 14)

*What really happened:* "About a week later, Sandeep's older sister Sumitha explained that her dad was really worried about Sandeep having a white girlfriend. I didn't agree with him, but I could see that Sandeep didn't want to make trouble at home. I went to see Mr Banerjee and explained that we were not boyfriend and girlfriend, just tennis partners. He said it was all right for us to play – and we won!"

Even with the best of friends, misunderstandings do happen and it is best to find out the facts first.

## 4. ALWAYS BE YOURSELF

Don't try to be someone you are not. If you try to be hilariously funny and crack endless jokes when you are not really a "punchline" sort of guy, you just end up looking stupid. Don't pretend to love outdoor pursuits like rock climbing or tramping for miles through rain-sodden woods if, in fact, your idea of fun is curling up with a good book.

And don't agree with everyone else just for the sake of it. Express your own opinions pleasantly and people will respect you for it – always say "Yes" just to keep in with the crowd and you will end up being known as someone with no opinions of their own.

Not sure exactly who you "yourself" are? Write a list of

everything you like doing and all your hopes and ambitions, and a second list of the things that really turn you off. Then write down the things that make you a good friend. For instance, your list could look like this:

*Likes* – tennis, table tennis, swimming, going to the cinema, bowling, making things, cooking.
*Dislikes* – team games, reading, puzzles of any kind, spending the evening in smoky discos, shopping and tidying my bedroom.
*Ambitions* – to be a dress designer, learn Thai cookery, get into the county table tennis squad.
*Things that scare me* – dogs, spiders, thunderstorms, walking into a room full of strangers, having to speak in public, lifts.
*Things I'm pretty good at* – keeping calm in a crisis, making and mending things, remembering people's birthdays and important dates, listening.

OK, you say. That's all very well. But supposing no-one wants to be my friend in the first place?

# BOOSTING YOUR CONFIDENCE

## REMEDY ONE: HOW TO OVERCOME SHYNESS

Shyness is a miserable feeling. Being shy:
(i) makes it harder to make friends
(ii) prevents you from standing up for your rights

(iii) hides all your good points from other people .

You think you are shy because you are frightened of other people. You're not. You are frightened of yourself: scared that you might say the wrong thing, use the wrong fork, not understand the jokes, wear the wrong gear. When you walk into a room, you are sure that it is going to be you that everyone stares at. But as a lady called Beth Day once said, "The world is not filled with strangers – it is full of other people waiting only to be spoken to." And that is what you have to do.

## 1. "BUT I FEEL SUCH AN IDIOT"

Accept that it is not your fault that you feel shy. No-one is going to punish you for it. You are not the only living soul ever to feel that way. Everyone feels shy sometimes, no matter how old they are and no matter how sophisticated they may seem. All those fears of walking into a room full of strangers, having people look at you and worrying about whether you are going red, are shared by thousands of others. The secret is not to let your shyness build a barrier between you and other people who could be your friends.

## 2. "BUT EVERYONE KEEPS LOOKING AT ME"

Forget about yourself. Stop imagining that the eyes of the world are on you. If you are shy, you imagine that everyone in the universe is looking at your laddered tights/criticising your dress sense/homing in on that spot three centimetres to the left of your right cheekbone. They're not – they are too busy trying to hide the stain on their waistcoat/pretend they know what Jemima Pinkerton is rabbiting on about/wishing they had plucked their eyebrows before they left home. Instead of worrying, look back at them with a broad smile and say, "Hi, I'm Matthew – I've just moved here from Kent. What goes on around here?"

3. *"BUT I ALWAYS GO BRIGHT RED "*
Everyone blushes at times. It's part of what is called the fear/anger response. We get ourselves into a state, so our body sends loads of blood to the surface of our skin to cool us down. It only lasts for a few seconds but the more you panic about it, the more likely it is to happen. It's a horrid feeling and it can happen in all sorts of different situations, whether it's being asked a tricky question in class or dropping your money all over the bus floor. If you feel it happening, a good ploy is to ask someone a question – while they are replying, you have time to get yourself together. Otherwise, just ignore it and carry on – chances are, no-one has noticed anyway.

4. *"BUT I NEVER KNOW WHAT TO SAY "*
Remember that when you are introduced to someone new, you are new to them too. They are probably standing there thinking, "Oh heavens, doesn't she look great in that outfit/She's the one who is brilliant at art/ Oh, what shall I talk about?" at just the same time that you are thinking "She's the girl who plays the trumpet so well/I wish I had chestnut hair/Oh, what shall I talk about?" If you concentrate on the fact that maybe they

are feeling shy and it is up to you to put them at their ease, you will forget your own shyness in next to no time.

### 5. *"BUT I DON'T KNOW ANY FUNNY JOKES"*
No problem. Trying to be clever, talking too loudly, bragging and telling silly jokes are all things people do to cover up feelings of insecurity. It doesn't work because people get bored with it all and drift off.

### 6. *"BUT I NEVER KNOW WHERE TO LOOK"*
Try the Don't Drop Code. Don't drop your head – gazing at your Reeboks makes you look unfriendly and it's hard for the other person to have a conversation with the top of your head. Don't drop your voice – speaking in a whisper only means that the other person will ask you to repeat what you said and you will have to go through the agony all over again. Don't drop your eyes – looking into someone's eyes makes you seem more approachable and gives the impression you're interested in them.

### 7. *"BUT I ALWAYS FEEL LIKE A NOBODY"*
Then play act. Some of the most famous actors and actresses are desperately shy – off-stage. But once they are in the limelight, they take on the character of the person they are playing. You can do it too. Don't stand around, arms folded, hugging your body, twiddling a strand of hair or wrapping one leg round the other. It looks as if you are deliberately cutting yourself off from everyone else and saying "I'm scared – go away." Instead, let your arms hang loosely by your side (that makes you

feel better too), use hand gestures, smile a lot and look interested. Act confident and you start to feel confident.

*BE PREPARED*
If you know that there are certain situations that make you particularly tongue-tied or embarrassed, it's worth working out a few strategies in advance.

Stephanie is 13. "My real dread is going into those communal changing rooms with all my friends. I always feel as if they are looking at me while I change – even if their backs are turned, they can see me in those huge mirrors. Then I worry because I am really flat-chested and I have loads of freckles on my back. The trouble is, the only shops we can all afford to buy clothes in don't have individual cubicles. What shall I do?"

*Strategy:* First of all, your friends probably know what you look like from gym and PE and swimming. And they will all be feeling paranoid about the way they look too – whether it's their big hips, the lack of a suntan or hammer toes – and because we British are nervous about looking at other people, everyone will have their eyes firmly on the floor or their own waistline anyway!

Lucy is 14. "My mum has said she will pay for me to have a new hairstyle for my next birthday but I am scared of going to the hairdresser. Last time I went, she cut it much shorter than I wanted, but I just couldn't bring myself to say anything. How can I pluck up the courage to be more in control?"

*Strategy:* Take a picture with you of the style you want and before she starts, say, "I want it exactly like this – if you don't think it will work, can you tell me now?" If you think she is cutting too much off, just say, "That's short enough now, thank you." A good ploy is to say something like "My friends don't bother going to the hairdressers because they can't find anyone to do it right – but if this works out, I'll tell them about you." They'll be doubly careful when they think more custom is on the way.

Alex is 13 and has been invited to Sunday lunch with her friend's parents. "The problem is that they are much better off than my family and live in a huge house and are quite posh. I'm scared that I won't know what to say, or that I'll pick up the wrong knife or spill something. What shall I do – say no to the invitation?"

*Strategy:* Don't turn down the chance to meet your friend's family. The thing to do is to offer to help carry dishes, play with the toddler, lay the table – anything to keep you busy and stop you worrying. You will go down a treat with your friend's mum who is probably in a dither because your friend's father hasn't made the gravy/ fetched grandma from the station/come in from the greenhouse yet. Most adults will strike up a conversation with you – the secret is to try to answer with something more than a monosyllabic "Yes" or "No". When friend's mum asks you, "Did you have a good time in France?", say something like "Yes – the food was incredible and we spent a lot of time on the river. Where did you go for your holiday?" They then launch into the saga of their fortnight in Benidorm and you don't have to say any more for ten minutes. When it comes to lunchtime, just watch what the others do and copy. Say something like "This casserole is really delicious, Mrs Gobsmacked," and you will be invited back again.

Alastair has a different problem. "I really enjoy English at school – except for Fridays. That day we all have to choose a poem, stand up and read it out in class. I go bright red, my mouth goes dry, my hands feel all clammy and I feel sick. My voice is breaking and it goes all squeaky and everyone titters. Even if I take the day off ill, I'll only be made to do it another day."

   *Strategy:* Putting it off just makes it worse – like going to the dentist. Choosing a funny poem helps because everyone laughs at the words, not you – and it makes you feel better. Or choose a poem you like and while you are reading it, listen to the words and imagine yourself in the poem. "I must go down to the sea again" (picture yourself hurtling along the sands at Blackpool), "Greasy Joan doth oil the pot" (dinner ladies in the canteen with polishing cloths). It does work, honestly. You may giggle, but it's better than feeling sick.


REMEDY TWO: WHO SAYS YOU ARE BORING?
"But even if I do pluck up the courage to talk to someone – I'm boring."

FACT: If you have been alive for ten years, you are not

boring. Think of all the things you have done, people you have met, places you have visited, hobbies you have been interested in. And then, when you have thought of them, keep quiet for a bit.

Remember, "A bore is someone who spends so much time talking about him or herself that you can't talk about yourself." So let the others chat about their holiday in Majorca, the sponsored bike ride or their new puppy. Ask them questions – what was the food like, what kind of bike do they have, what is the puppy called? Chances are they will start asking you questions, and hey presto! you discover that you are not boring at all. If they do just carry on talking about themselves, then they will have had a good time and think you're interesting – just because you listened to them! And in this case, you are entitled to think they are boring!

## REMEDY THREE: THERE'S MORE TO LIFE THAN TENNIS
"But even if I do make a friend, I'm useless at sports."

There is a myth going round that to be a Popular Person you have to spend your weekends dripping wet upside down in a canoe, or caked in mud and covered with bruises on a rugby pitch. Balderdash. If your friend is into hurling himself around at high speed in the fog and snow, good luck to him. You can always stand on the sidelines with a flask of hot chocolate, five scarves and fur-lined boots and cheer him on. Or wait at home with the kettle on. And before you write yourself off as being "useless" at games, remember that not many sports actually feature at school. You could have the potential to become an ace darts player, ice skating queen, or wizard with the snooker cue. Give it a go. And don't forget that all those athletic types need someone to keep score, hand out the Lucozade and write up the results in the school newsletter. It could be you.

## REMEDY FOUR: BEAUTY IS IN THE EYE OF THE BEHOLDER

"But no-one is going to want me as a friend – I'm ugly/ fat/spotty."

Just listen to this little lot: "I have eyes like those of a dead pig"; "My face looks like a wedding cake that has been left out in the rain"; "I guess I look like a rock quarry that someone has dynamited."

These self-deprecating remarks were made by Marlon Brando (who was an utterly gorgeous film star years back), W H Auden (a very clever poet) and Charles Bronson, who starred in more Westerns than you've had Big Macs, which just goes to show that everyone, even the rich and famous and disgustingly successful, think they look peculiar. Slim people moan about the shape of their noses or think their hips are too bony, people with faces like goddesses complain about their flabby thighs. If you are blonde with blue eyes, you want to be dark with green eyes and if you are short for your age, you are convinced that all your problems would disappear overnight if only you could grow three inches.

Look at your schoolmates. How many of them are model material? How many could you see strutting down the catwalks of Paris and Milan? How many are so stunning that they should be on the cover of a glossy magazine? But they are still have friends, don't they? People didn't say, "Well, she's really friendly and great to be with but of course, I can't be her friend because her bottom is too big and one of her front teeth is crooked." And no-one is going to say that about you.

If you are overcome by embarrassment about your appearance – don't be so self-absorbed. Do you honestly believe that the rest of the world is spending its time looking at you? They are not. They are too busy looking at themselves.

And if you really hate your appearance, think of ways to improve it. If you feel your clothes are all wrong, tell your parents how unhappy you feel and ask if you could have some money to buy a few more hip outfits, or if you could have some for your next birthday. If your hair is lank and lifeless, think about getting a really good cut and restyle. If spots are the problem, see your doctor – modern science has come up with some pretty effective spot creams that can zap acne at 20 paces.

## Chapter 3

# GETTING FRIENDS, KEEPING FRIENDS

*"A man should keep his friendship in constant repair."*
Dr Samuel Johnson

It's one thing working out what a Real Friend is, and listing all the ways we can be sure that we are in the running for Number One Ally of the Decade, and quite another keeping those precious friends once we have found them. Friendship doesn't just happen; it needs working at, nurturing and looking after. And just as you think you have got the knack of it, it changes. We never stop learning about relationships or trying to get them right, no matter how old we are.

## SIX SURE-FIRE WAYS TO FRIGHTEN AWAY POTENTIAL FRIENDS

1. Spend the first few hours after meeting someone new talking about yourself. Tell them how great you are at soccer, how your mum and dad own Northamptonshire and how you think anyone who can't get to the final frame of Sonic 3 in 20 minutes is a dimbo.

2. Borrow something from them and forget to give it back. Great route to friendship this, especially if, when they finally coerce you into returning the item, it is torn/cracked/covered in peanut butter.

3. Be unbearably possessive. The moment they start to be friends with anyone else, sulk, whinge, stamp your foot and threaten never to speak to them again. Refuse to include their other friends in anything you do and spend all the time you are together running down everyone they know.

4. When your new friend trusts you enough to tell you something in confidence, promise faithfully never to

repeat a single syllable to a living soul and then go and tell the whole of Year Eleven and the queue at the bus stop.

5. Be all over them when you need them and drop them like a hot brick when they stop being useful. After all, you only wanted them because they had a swimming pool/sexy older brother/free pass to Ritzies Night Club, didn't you?

6. Pinch their boyfriend/girlfriend. This is the quickest way to lose a friend and it simply *is not done*. That's not to say that the boy or girl who is currently going out with your friend won't one day decide he or she prefers you – but until that day dawns, it is definitely *hands off*! If in doubt, just pause to consider how you would feel if someone stole your beloved.

7. Be pushy. Impose all your ideas on your new-found friend, demand to spend all your time with them and telephone them every 30 minutes all weekend to check they still like you.

## SIX SURE-FIRE WAYS TO MAKE A NEW FRIEND WANT TO HANG AROUND

1. Be interested in them. Everyone, but everyone, adores talking about their favourite topic. Themselves – their boyfriends, family, hopes, fears – it doesn't mater what.

Just show that you are interested in what they feel and think is important, and you are halfway there.

2. Accept them for what they are, warts and all. They may have different tastes in clothes to you, come from a different background and talk with a different accent. They may even live in a house with a lilac front door and three dozen gnomes in the front garden, but none of those things makes them odd/substandard/crazy (well, the gnomes maybe ...). Part of the fun of having friends is sharing different ideas and getting to know different lifestyles – and anyway, they probably think your tank of piranha fish and the 14 white mice in a cage on the landing are pretty odd.

3. Have a laugh. Gustave Flaubert, who was a frightfully clever French writer who lived 100 years ago, said, "A laughing man is stronger than a suffering man." What he meant was that, if you laugh when something goes wrong or you put your foot in it, you are more likely to come through in one piece. So when someone pulls your leg, or giggles when you get your French future perfect in a twist, laugh out loud. You'll feel better and they will love you for it. Laughing at yourself is a sure way to be friendly – laughing at others is not. And remember, if your friend is trying to be funny it is kinder to laugh than to say, "I suppose you think that was a good joke – well, it was pathetic."

4. Ask their advice. Everyone loves to feel important and

there is no better way to get the ball rolling than to say something like "I hear you are brilliant at electronics. How do you think I should wire up my speakers for the party?" or "Could you hear me say my lines for *Twelfth Night* and give me a few tips? – you're pretty good at drama." You don't have to be all gushing and nauseous about it – just make the other person feel good.

5. Be nice to their friends and family. It is a fact of life that parents in general, and mothers in particular, nag their kids something rotten if they consider their friends are rude/scruffy/self-centred. Making a good impression may sound ultra-boring but it's time well spent. OK, so Carole's mum goes on a bit and her gran shouts because she is deaf and keeps calling you "girl" because she can't remember your name, but it won't hurt you to smile, say thank you from time to time and offer to make a cup of tea. It will be worth it when you and Carole want a night out and her mum says "yes" because you are "such a nice girl and a good influence"!

6. Make an effort with them. Don't keep accepting invitations round to their house without inviting them back. Take it in turns to telephone each other – don't expect them to foot the bill all the time. And make sure that you find out what they enjoy doing and don't always call the tune yourself.

# VARIETY IS THE SPICE OF LIFE

The great thing about friends is that they come in all shapes and sizes. You have friends you play badminton with who wouldn't want to come on holiday with you; friends you go to discos with but who would hate a shopping trip to London. Friendship, like everything else in life, comes in many varieties. There are people you really like and whose company you enjoy, but whom you don't have enough in common with to ever get really close. Don't push it – the sort of friend you see once in a while for a day out has just as much to offer as your bosom pal.

# GROUPS

Some kids, when they first break away from their parents, choose to go around in groups. Others prefer to know just a few people really well. There is no right or wrong way – it depends what you enjoy most. Boys, in particular, often choose to be part of a group – possibly because they all share a common interest such as football or potholing or mountain biking which they can all do together. Girls often like to discuss their emotions and feelings, which is more easily done with just one or two other people.

## WHAT'S SO GREAT ABOUT GROUPS?

### 1. *YOU FEEL SAFE*
Being part of a group helps you make that transition from going around with your mum and dad and brothers and sisters and going it alone.

### 2. *YOU GET A FEELING OF SELF-WORTH*
The great thing about a group of kids your own age is that they are feeling as uncertain and confused about Life, Love and the Pursuit of Dreams as you are. You all want to try out new ideas and exchange new thoughts. With friends, you get to explore a whole different set of values from the ones your parents hold. That doesn't mean your friends are right and your parents are wrong – or vice versa. But sometimes it is good to discover different ways of looking at the same things.

### 3. *IF ONE PERSON TEASES YOU, CHANCES ARE, ONE OF THE OTHERS WILL BE ON YOUR SIDE*
At home, let's face it, Dad is likely to say things like "You don't know what you are talking about ... " or Grandpa will mutter, "When I was a lad, I knew my place ... " With friends, you can air your views without anyone telling you that you haven't sufficient experience to express an opinion.

### 4. *YOU SHARE THE SAME INTERESTS*
Most groups start from a mutual liking of something – football, music, mountain bikes. Some just start because

you all enjoy talking and thrashing out new ideas about style, clothes, behaviour and the opposite sex. The world is changing fast, and however hard your parents try to keep pace with new ideas, technology and outlooks, they are one generation removed from the action. With a group your own age, you get a sense of belonging and you learn to listen to other people's points of view.

## 5. *YOU HAVE SOME READY ANSWERS TO ALL THOSE PERPLEXING QUESTIONS*

You know the sort of things – "What should I be wearing?", "Who's the lead singer of the Muskrats?", "Should we do something to stop them building that new road through the common?" Parents rarely share their kids' tastes in clothes, music or humour and it is good to be surrounded by people who appreciate what you do – without telling you to "Turn that racket off", "Take that muck off your face" or "Grow up!"

## 6. *YOU LEARN TO MIX WITH LOTS OF DIFFERENT TYPES OF PEOPLE*

Sometimes you have to put others in the group first and sometimes they will put you first. Sometimes you will be the leader, at other times the follower.

## 7. *YOU LEARN TO ACCEPT A NEW SET OF RULES AND TAKE NOTICE OF WHAT OTHER PEOPLE THINK OF YOU*

Your mum and dad probably think you are the most amazing/prettiest/cleverest child ever born, but your friends are likely to take a more realistic view.

Rachel is 13 and goes around in a group of six friends ranging in age from 12 to 14. "At home, I can't argue about politics or what's happening in Bosnia because my dad always interrupts and says I am too young to know what I am talking about. With my friends, I can say how I feel and know that even if I am wrong, they will hear me out."

Katya is 14, and last year turned vegetarian. She is keen on animal rights and is into recycling and other ecological issues. "When I told my mum I wanted to be vegetarian, she went mad and said I wouldn't get enough vitamins for a growing teenager and that it would just be more work for her. And my dad is always teasing me about the posters I make protesting against things like fox-hunting and drug testing on animals. But my friends really understand and they all back me up – even the ones who eat meat. With my friends I feel that my ideas count for something."

Vince is an only child of 13, living with his mum and grandmother since his dad left home. "I really love my mum and gran but they get really upset when I argue with them. I don't mean about house rules and stuff but things like having student councils at school and giving kids a bigger say in things that affect them. Whatever I say, my mum tells me I haven't a clue about life or anything else for that matter. So I shut up and talk about it to my friends."

## WHAT'S NOT SO GREAT ABOUT GROUPS?

Like everything else in life, being part of a group can have
its down side. It's possible to spend such a lot of time
worrying that you might get dumped by the gang that
you never really enjoy being part of it. And if you find
yourself doing things you don't feel happy with just to
keep in with them, it's time to split. If the group is a big
one, you can end up not knowing any member really well.
You can also find yourself always giving in to the most
noisy, pushy or vociferous members of the group and
being pushed into the background.

## ARE YOU A GOOD GROUPY?

Being a group member has its own responsibilities and
pitfalls. How do you rate?

1. Every Friday, someone in the group has everyone
round to their house to watch videos or play CDs. This
week it's your turn but your mum has a migraine and
says you must cancel. Do you:
(a) Shout at her, call her names, slam a few doors for
good measure and tell your friends that your mum is a
spoilsport and don't they feel sorry for you?
(b) Tell your friends that your mum has just been made
vice-president of her firm and you have to go with her to
the celebration cocktail party?
(c) Tell them the truth and offer to take the pizzas and

drinks that you were going to serve, round to someone else's house instead?

2. For weeks, you and Pippa and Kirsty and Sophie have been looking forward to going to the rock concert in town. A few days before, Kirsty is taken ill and has to go to hospital. Do you:
(a) Think "That's her tough luck," sell her ticket and divide the proceeds between you?
(b) Sell her ticket and give her the money?
(c) Sell her ticket, give her the money and club together for a video of the concert as well?

3. One evening you are walking through the park with your friends when you see a little kid crying. He looks as if he is on his own. Do you:
(a) Suggest you find out if he is OK – but when your friends say you will be late for the film, you shrug your shoulders and go on with them?
(b) Tell them you will catch them up but that you want to check it out?
(c) Persuade one of them to come with you and another to phone the police just in case the child has been reported missing?

4. Every Tuesday evening, you baby-sit your next door neighbour's little girl while the neighbour goes to visit her mother in hospital. One Tuesday, the group decide to go to the new wave pool in town. Do you:
(a) Say "Sorry, but Tuesday is a bad night for me – have a

great time"?

(b) Ring your neighbour and say you have come down with a streaming cold – and then go swimming?

(c) Suggest they go on Wednesday instead and then sulk when they say that Wednesday is bad for them?

*ANSWERS*

1. (a) 0. It's bad enough yelling at your mum when she feels rough but you don't have to run her down to your friends as well.

(b) 0. Why lie? You will get found out and no-one will trust you next time.

(c) 5. Offering to do the food stops anyone else having to rush round organising things and proves that you were not trying to get out of your responsibilities.

2. (a) 0. Cheating your friends is the lowest trick of all.

(b) 5. The honourable thing – it is her ticket, after all.

(c) 5. A nice gesture if you can afford it.

3. (a) 0. Keeping in with the gang is all very well but that could be your kid brother – and it's always better to be safe than sorry.

(b) 3. Very sensible but probably best to see (c) below.

(c) 5. Taking someone else with you is a safety precaution and phoning the police means that if something is wrong, help is on the way as fast as possible. Don't jump to conclusions, though: if the little lad's mum is sunbathing behind the cafe, they won't thank you for calling out three panda cars and a fire engine.

4. (a) 5. You are not stopping the rest from going and you are not letting anyone down.

(b) 2. You might get away with it – but then again, you might not and where is your credibility then? And what about your neighbour's mum stuck in hospital and longing for a visitor?

(c) 0. The rest of the world does not have to fit in with you.

# BEST FRIENDS

Going around in a group is great – but often you start to find that you are spending more and more time with one person and soon you have that invaluable asset – A Best Friend.

## WHAT MAKES A FRIEND INTO A BEST FRIEND?

1. A best friend is usually the same sex as you and round about the same age.

2. A best friend is someone you can share your innermost thoughts and feelings with and they will share theirs with you. You can talk about absolutely everything from pop music to field sports, from animal rights to dyeing your hair purple.

3. A best friend shares experiences. When something

awful happens to you, they hurt too. And when they win top prize in the Dance Marathon or get chosen as Carnival Princess, you buy the pizzas and the Dr Pepper.

4. A best friend is there for the bad times as well as the good. They stand by you when you get punished for something you haven't done, hold your hand while you throw up after experimenting with scrumpy cider, and come to the funeral of your pet hamster.

5. A best friend is someone you feel so close to that you never have to pretend.

6. A best friend knows that your mum has a thing about shoes being taken off inside the house, no cats on the bed and no naughty words in front of your father, and behaves accordingly.

7. A best friend can last you a lifetime.


## HAVE YOU GOT WHAT IT TAKES TO BE A BEST FRIEND?

1. Your best friend Kate has promised to come over after supper to help you highlight your hair. At 9.30 pm she still hasn't turned up and when you phone, she just says something cropped up and puts the phone down. Do you:
(a) Ring back, tell her she is a heartless beast and vow never to speak to her again?

(b) Ring round all your other friends and tell them that Kate is an unreliable pig and make them promise to ignore her at school tomorrow?
(c) See her first thing the next morning and ask her what happened?

2. Every weekend, you and your best friend Vicki go to the shopping mall, have a burger and go to a film. Suddenly Vicki says she doesn't want to come any more. Do you:
(a) Say "Please yourself" and forget her?
(b) Ask her whether there is something else she would rather do?
(c) Say "If you don't come, I won't be your friend any more?"

3. You really like your friend Helen but your mum says she is tired of waiting on her hand and foot whenever she comes round to your house. Do you:
(a) Call your mum old-fashioned and a nag, storm upstairs and sulk for the rest of the day?
(b) Phone Helen and say, "My mum hates you so you had better not come round again?"
(c) Carry on as normal but drag Helen into the kitchen the following Saturday, saying, "I thought we'd make the omelettes for tea this week – and let's ask Mum if she'd like one as well?"

4. You and your best friend have always told each other everything. Suddenly she goes all silent on you, stops

phoning and looks really miserable at school. Do you:
(a) Say "If you are going to be moody, I'm going to go round with Val"?
(b) Catch her after school and say "I can't help noticing that you seem a bit down – is there anything I can do?"
(c) Ignore her?

5. After half-term, there is a new boy in your class. You get really friendly with him but the rest of your friends don't want to include him in the group's activities. Do you:
(a) Find out why they don't want him in the gang and say that you think they are not giving him a fair chance?
(b) Think, "If they don't like him, there must be something wrong with him and I'd better give him the push"?
(c) Go on being friendly and introduce him to lots of other people as well?

*ANSWERS*
1. (a) Silly. With a bit of luck, she will know you did this in a fit of pique – but she might just decide to take you at your word.

   (b) 0. Stupid. Why make yourself look selfish and bad-tempered? – and anyway, you know the facts.

   (c) 5. Sensible. Once you do know the facts, you can decide how to act.

2. (a) 2. Unkind. You can't think that much of her if you let her go that easily – and she might need your support.

(b) 5. Understanding. It gives her a chance to say she is too hard up to go shopping/prefers to play tennis with her cousin/is grounded by her dad for answering back once too often.

(c) 0. Pathetic. Trading off favours is not what Real Friends do.

3. (a) 1. Pointless. If it's your mum who is slaving away cooking tea, vacuuming carpets and persuading your father to clear up his newspapers, she deserves to be able to express her point of view. The only reason you get one point for this is because if you are upstairs being a jerk, your mum gets a bit of peace and quiet.

(b) 0. Untruthful. Your mum never said whether she liked Helen or not – just that she didn't like waiting on her.

(c) 5. Right on. You get in with your mum, who views you as something of a saint for the next week and doubles your allowance, Helen gets to see the inside of a kitchen, and you get to put double sweetcorn and treble chicken in your omelette before anyone can say no.

4. (a) Insensitive. People are usually quiet for a reason and they cannot guarantee to be permanently sunny and jolly just because you want it that way. And to hear that at the first sign of trouble you ditch her for Val won't help to cheer her up.

(b) 5. If she wants to talk, she can. If not, she still knows that you care.

(c) 2. Better than (a) but hurtful – and by the way, how

would you feel if she ignored you on the day your gerbil died/your brother smashed your best CD/your dad got fired from his job?

5. (a) 5. This gives your friends the chance to think again and shows that you are not always influenced by their opinions.

    (b) 0. Being new at school is hard – and to have the person who has just made friends with you disappear overnight makes things even harder.

    (c) 4. The more people you introduce him to, the greater his chances of finding a real mate.


## BUT EVEN BEST FRIENDS HAVE THEIR MOMENTS

If one of your gang does something you don't like, or says something you think is completely idiotic, chances are you will shrug your shoulders, think "How stupid" and carry on chatting with one of the others. But when your best friend, your soulmate, that extra-special person, starts acting in ways you find difficult to take, it is a different matter.

  But just how do you get your point across without causing a humdinger of a row or tears all round? A lot depends on how far you think friends can go. Would you:

(i)  Tell your friend she had bad breath?

(ii)  Tell your friend she had BO?

(iii) Tell your friend that his new girlfriend was a two-timing so-and-so who was seeing Pete behind his back?

(iv)  Tell your friend that the new outfit she has just spent two months' allowance on is utterly hideous, makes her look fat and doesn't suit her complexion?
(v)   Repeat to your friend all the nasty things that other kids were saying about him behind his back?

*IF YOU SAID "YES" TO ALL THE QUESTIONS*
Well, you're honest, I'll give you that. But while there are some things that friends can tell one another fairly safely (provided they put it nicely), there are others which are best left unsaid. Telling your friend he has body odour or that his breath smells is very important, but you should do it kindly. Say something like "I reckon you didn't have time to take a shower after basketball – do you want to borrow my deodorant?" – not "Golly, you stink again!" But if your best friend has been working herself silly, mowing her dad's lawn and baby-sitting the next-door neighbour's twins in order to save up for a new pair of crushed velvet leggings and a silk shirt, telling her she looks frightful is really tricky. You don't want to sound mean but you would hate her to make the same mistake again. You could say "Those leggings are great – have you thought of getting a pair in black instead of the pale primrose? Shall we go to FrillyFings again and see whether they will do a swap?" Of course, you must also remember that it could be just you who thinks she looks awful. Someone else might consider that she looks a million dollars.

As for telling a friend that someone has been saying horrid things behind their back, it very much depends what is being said. If it is just meanminded jeering, ignore it. If, on the other hand, people have misunderstood something your friend has done – the reason they won't play sport or refuse to go to the swimming pool, for instance – a quiet word might give your friend the chance to set the record straight. Or be a real friend and sort it out quietly yourself.

The great rule is never intend to *hurt* – but always set out to *help*.

## OTHER SORTS OF FRIENDS

### THE ONCE-IN-A-WHILE FRIEND

Just as most of us have a best friend, nearly everyone has a few friends that they only see once in a while. It might be because they used to live close by and then one moved away; sometimes it's because they have developed different interests and only meet up occasionally. But it needn't make the friendship any less important.

"I went ice-skating with Laura for three years and we got on really well. But she was much better at it than I was and went on to enter competitions and represent the club all over the country. Now I hardly ever see her because skating is her life. But she sends me postcards when she goes away and phones me once a month and when we do see each other, it's like we have never been apart. I still count her as one of my really good friends." (Maddie, aged 13)

"I was really good mates with Grant till his dad got moved to Scotland by his firm. At first, we phoned each other a lot, but our parents moaned about the phone bill so we started writing. Now we send letters about once a month and in the summer Grant is coming down to stay. I miss him a lot – we used to play for the same cricket team and go biking together – but I guess we will just pick up again." (Sean, aged 14)

"I used to be best friends with Claire and then she got really ill and had to spend weeks in hospital. At first I went to see her every Friday after school but, to be honest, I used to feel all shaky and queasy seeing her wired up to tubes and things and I stopped going. I felt awful about that so I wrote letters and sent her magazines and things. Anyway, she got better and started to come to school for the mornings only. I was really worried that she would hate me for not going to see her more often but she seemed to understand. She still likes me, but I am not sure I like myself much for not making more of an effort to overcome my fear of hospitals for her sake." (Gaby, aged 15)

The thing about all these friendships is that they didn't become less important because the people involved saw each other less; in fact they stayed strong despite all sorts of problems. When Laura's love of skating took her all over the country, she still kept in touch with Maddie; when Grant moved to Scotland, he didn't ditch Sean because the distance was so great; and when Claire was in hospital Gaby sent her letters and magazines even though she didn't visit. What is more, Claire didn't hold Gaby's fear of hospitals against her.

## THE FAMILY FRIEND

Family get-togethers can be hideously dreary, especially when your mother wants you to wear "something respectable" – which usually means not your torn jeans, paisley waistcoat and Doc Martens. You squirm at the thought of all the aunts asking you if you are enjoying school and saying "My, haven't you grown!" (since they last saw you three years ago, it would be pretty worrying if you hadn't). You have to make polite conversation to your granddad (who can't hear a word you are saying anyway) and eat Aunt Muriel's sausage rolls that are all roll and no sausage. Boring, or what?

But just once in a while, the family throws up someone who turns out to be a real mate. That happened to Caroline.

"I had never taken much notice of my cousin Richard. He's five years older than me and at university in Sussex. But when my grandfather had his 80th birthday party, we got talking and he is really nice. He didn't laugh when I said I wanted to be a foreign correspondent like Kate Adie (my dad always says things like "What, you who screams in a thunderstorm?") and he said he would lend me books about courses in journalism. Sure enough, about a week later this parcel arrived with loads of information in it and when we met up again at my parents' silver wedding party, he asked me how my plans were going."

For Benedict, it was a family christening that started a really good friendship for him. "I am really keen on archery but since we moved to our new town, there isn't a club nearby for me to join so I don't get to do it much. At the christening, my aunt introduced me to one of the godparents and it turned out that he was an archery fanatic! We talked for ages and in the end he organised for me to get some lessons from a friend of his. What's more, I go over to his house sometimes – he has targets on the lawn and he lets me practise."

Another bonus with family friends is that a lot of them have known your family for a long time. When things go wrong, it is these friends who rally round to save the day. That happened to Paula and her brother.

"My mum has been friends with Jennifer for years. They used to go to school together and Jennifer comes to stay every Easter. Last year, my mum got cancer and me and my brother were really scared. Dad was at the hospital a lot and Jenny moved in to help look after us. She was really good – she sat for hours talking to us and explaining about Mum's illness. We know Mum will be ill for a long time and having Jenny to talk things over with helps us both a lot."

## OLDER FRIENDS

It's quite possible to have a good friend who is years older than you. Beverley was really fed up when her mother asked her to visit their elderly neighbour who had come out of hospital after a hip replacement operation and whose family lived too far away to visit her.

"She's really old – her grandchildren are older than I am – and I thought it would be deadly. But I had a brilliant time. She has this amazing collection of old postcards of our town and tins full of newspaper cuttings from the war. She's going to help me with my history project – and teach me how to make flapjacks!"

## PENFRIENDS

Striking up a pen friendship with someone overseas can be a rip-roaring success or an unmitigated disaster – but until you give it a go, you never know which it will turn out to be. Schoolteachers love you to write to kids your own age in France or Germany because they think it will improve your linguistic skills. (What they don't realise is that you persuade Mr Leacroft next door, who speaks fluent everything, to tell you what to put.) Parents like it because they think that with a bit of luck they will get to pack you off to Marseilles or Frankfurt for half the summer and get their bathroom and telephone back. But from your point of view, it is not always easy. Christine had been writing to Marie-Louise in Marseilles for two years and then went to stay for three weeks.

"It was awful – I was so homesick and I was embarrassed about anyone seeing me in tears. I hated the food – there was lots of oil and dressings – and they drank wine with their meals and talked to each other really fast in French which I couldn't understand. Marie-Louise tried to translate at first but she soon got bored with it and every mealtime was a nightmare. I would never go again."

But for Jack it worked out brilliantly. "My penfriend Frederick lives in Frankfurt and I spent two weeks there last summer. I was a bit nervous because although I knew from his letters that he enjoyed soccer and table tennis like me, his house looked really huge and I was worried about fitting in with his family. When I got there it turned out that the house was divided into apartments and he lived in one of them! I loved the German food and Frederick's parents were really friendly. Next Easter he is coming to stay with me in London."

## FRIENDS OF THE OPPOSITE SEX

When you were at playgroup, you had friends who were girls and friends who were boys. Nobody thought twice if Toby was playing houses with Rosie, or Sally was building a space rocket with Martin. As you got older, the girls tended to hang around together and the boys followed suit. This wasn't a bad idea – girls seem to grow up faster than boys and enjoy doing things in twos and threes, while most of the games boys play require loads of people and half an acre of mud to play it on.

Then one day, round about the age of 11 or 12, something odd happens. You suddenly notice that Jake, who has lived next door for years and who wouldn't let you play on his Nintendo, really does have the most gorgeous eyes and when he smiles at you, your knees go all wobbly and you get prickles down the back of your neck.

Around the same time, your cousin Dave – the one who last Christmas was saying that girls were wet and romance was soppy – appears to be going to great lengths to win the admiration of your friend Alison. He even offers to help her with her science project, which for someone who used to dodge homework like the bubonic plague marks a major transformation.

You and Dave have discovered – well, what have you discovered?

*IS IT LOVE?*
Hard to say. Just because a boy is attracted to a girl who looks good, is fun to be with and happens to have a pretty brill video games collection, does not mean that he loves her. Only time will tell that. And just because you spend three hours getting ready to go to school just in case Jake sits next to you on the bus doesn't mean you are in love – it means you think he is attractive and you want him to think the same about you.

75

### IS IT JUST A STATUS SYMBOL?
There comes a time when your friend Mandy and your friend Carole and your friend Rowena are all talking about their boyfriends and you want one too. It's like the time when you were in the First Form and everyone was getting yo-yos – you didn't feel part of the crowd until you had one as well. It happens to boys as well, although usually a bit later than to girls. Suddenly all their friends are skipping footie practice to meet a girlfriend – and they feel out of it because they are still more interested in goal kicks than girls. That's fine – there is no written rule that says you have to have a girlfriend or boyfriend at a certain age. Some people have their first romance at 13, others still haven't felt the need by the time they reach Year Twelve. Both are perfectly normal.

### IS IT LUST?
Your body is changing apace, and by golly it makes its presence felt at times. Bits of you that you forgot you had, start behaving as though they had a mind of their own and sometimes it all feels so good that you want to do something about it. But sex is not just a cheap thrill to be experienced as soon as possible, and to have a friend of the opposite sex just because you want to "see what IT is like" is stupid. Sex should be the ultimate expression of a relationship that has grown slowly – not a quick method of impressing your mates.

### OR IS IT JUST ANOTHER FRIENDSHIP?
Funnily enough, all the rules and guidelines to being a

good friend apply whether that friend is of the same sex or not. Caring about someone means wanting them to be happy, safe, protected, cherished and respected. And building a solid friendship is the thing that matters more than anything. Love, romance, and a lasting relationship may follow but if it doesn't you've still got another good mate – and all the time in the world to fall in love.

The most irritating thing about a friendship with someone of the opposite sex is that loads of people will assume you are "going out" or are passionately in love with one another. Just because Shaun is friendly with Annabel doesn't mean she is his girlfriend, and because Gail spends a lot of time with Ian doesn't mean she is in love. If only it were that simple. First you have to deal with the parents.

*Mother:* "You're seeing a lot of that Tim – you are too young to have a boyfriend."
*Julie:* "He's not a boyfriend, Mum – he's just a friend who happens to be a boy."
*Mother:* "Yes, well that's as may be, but I'm not having you two up in that bedroom of yours alone."
*Julie:* "But Mum, all we are doing is playing records."
*Mother:* "Well, play them in the sitting-room then."

Sounds familiar? Your mother is worried. Why?

1. She's heard your friend Melanie say that you are "going out" with Tim. She doesn't understand that this means you are seen by your friends as a pair – not that

you are about to leap into bed with one another.

2. This is just another indication that you are growing up fast and that one day soon, you will be an independent woman. She is proud – but she is sad and scared too that you might get hurt.

3. She remembers what it is like to be young and she worries that, despite your assurances, your emotions might get too strong for you to handle.

Talk to your mum. Explain that you know the risks, that you are responsible and that you and Tim really are "just good friends". Tell her that you like Tim because of his sense of humour and interest in jazz and that you regard him in the same way as your girl friends. If you do feel more for Tim then talk about the best way to handle these new feelings.

*KEEP YOUR OTHER FRIENDS*
Even if you're desperately in love you shouldn't ditch your old friends. Claire and Mandy lived in the same village and had been friends for years. Then Steve moved into the bungalow next door to Mandy and they started going around together. Suddenly Claire found that Mandy no longer wanted to play badminton, go shopping or even sit with her on the bus. When Claire had 'flu, Mandy didn't even ring to see how she was. Claire was really unhappy about it, but she had other friends and as the weeks went by she started seeing them regularly. Within a

month or two, she had a new best friend. But then Steven found another girlfriend and Mandy wanted Claire back to herself again. She seemed surprised to discover that Claire had a new best friend whom she didn't want to lose. Mandy had lost out.

## FORCED TO MAKE NEW FRIENDS: PACK UP YOUR STUFF – WE'RE MOVING
### (and you don't need to take those posters)

Back in the mists of antiquity, when families were born, raised, married and buried in the same village, no-one had the hassle of having to make friends. You grew up with the same people, had measles and scurvy with them and probably ended up marrying one of them. By the time you were grown up, you knew all there was to know about everyone in the community. But these days, things don't work like that.

There you are, happily jogging along at school, swimming for the Under 15s and pretty certain to be chosen to play Pharaoh in the school production of *Joseph and the Amazing Technicolour Dreamcoat* – and wham! your father comes home one Friday night, all pink about the gills from his celebratory session at the Pickled Goose and Gobstopper, and says, "I got the job! We move to Lymm in two weeks' time!"

Lymm? Lymm? Where on earth is Lymm? Out on a limb, more like. No way. You are not going. This is definite.

They cannot be so cruel. You will ring Childline. You will run away. No, no, *no*! Then they chat you up with the "There's a lovely school, dear, and the Head seemed very nice." Never mind the school and sucks to the Head. "*What about my friends?*" So they sit you down and have a little chat.

## WHAT YOUR PARENTS SAY AND WHAT YOU SAY

"You'll make other friends." — "I want the ones I've got now."

"You can keep in touch and they can come and stay." — "It's not the same – I want to see them every day."

"Think how exciting it will be to meet new people." — "No it won't – it will be scary and embarrassing and lonely."

So how easy is it to move away from everything and everyone you know and start afresh? Not easy – but not as hard as you think it is right now. So who's right?

1. *"YOU'LL MAKE OTHER FRIENDS"*
Right. The fact that you have friends now means that you are the sort of person that people enjoy being with. No matter where you go, from Manchester to Mullingar, or Ipswich to Inverness, people have the same needs. They may speak with a different accent, eat black pudding and

Eccles cakes or wade knee-deep in icy rivers catching trout for tea, but they are all human beings looking for other human beings to be friends with.

## 2. *"BUT I WANT THE ONES I'VE GOT NOW AND I WANT TO SEE THEM EVERY DAY"*

The ones who are Real Friends will go on being Real Friends. Seeing someone every day is no guarantee of continuing friendship – look at all the mates you have fallen out with over the past two years and they were under your very nose (which is partly why you fell out with them). You can write, phone (choose cheap rate times – it saves the parents turning purple once a quarter when the phone bill arrives), visit one another at half-term and during the holidays – and you will be surprised to find that after you have been together again for about three and a half minutes, it will be as if you have never been apart. The friends you *might* lose touch with are the Fair-weather Friends – the ones who were always around when you had a birthday party or were handing out the Continental Chocolate Assortment, but never when you had a nose bleed in Chemistry or felt sick at the bus station. And if you think about it, they are no great loss.

## 3. *"YOU CAN KEEP IN TOUCH AND THEY CAN COME TO STAY"*

See? Even your parents, who are leaping about surrounded by packing cases and bubble-wrap, all flushed with excitement at the thought of a pay rise, company car and the excuse for new duvet covers, have had time to realise that you are not greeting this great adventure with quite the same degree of enthusiasm. They know they will be footing the bill for stamps and phone calls, driving to stations to pick up friends and subbing you £20 for the coach fare to Alice's disco. They know how hard it is for you to move and they want to soften the blow as much as possible. They will spoil you for a while, but of course, you won't be interested in that, will you?

4. *"THINK HOW EXCITING IT WILL BE TO MEET NEW PEOPLE." "NO, IT WON'T ... ETC ETC "*
You are both right. At first, it will seem as if only you are right. Meeting new people is a bit scary and you can bet that on the first day that your dad starts his new job, he won't be able to eat his cornflakes, will reverse the car into a bush and blame your mother, and feel ever so slightly sick as he walks into the office. By the end of the first week, he will be playing golf with Alec from Accounts, lunching with Edward from Exports and talking about the place as if he had been there for years. And it will be the same for you.

## STARTING OVER

When you start a new school, you will feel lost, sick and totally unable to eat your usual Ready Brek and chopped banana. So what can you do to make life easier?

## 1. *DON'T CRITICISE*

Saying "We didn't do it that way at Featherstone High," or "Our gym was much bigger and better than this dump," is not the way to endear yourself to your new friends. They can call their gym a dump – you can't. Not yet.

## 2. *DON'T BE AFRAID TO ASK QUESTIONS*

If you don't know the way to the Art Block, or what you are supposed to do at lunchtime, go up to someone who looks friendly and ask. If you can choose someone who is on their own, so much the better. The chances are they will stay with you for the rest of the day.

## 3. *DON'T BRAG*

It's not a good idea to march into your first French lesson and say, "I won the languages prize three years in a row so yah boo sucks to you lot." Conversely, it's a clever move to ask someone who looks approachable for help over something – "I've never been very good at Science – how do you get this Bunsen burner to light?"

## 4. *SUSS OUT THE OTHER KIDS BUT DON'T JUDGE TOO SOON*

You need not worry about *no-one* speaking to you because in every class there is a Kenneth King Pin and Bella Queen Bee who will rush up and want to know everything about you from your shoe size and waist measurement to where you spent your holidays and the contents of your lunchbox. Then there will be the Hearty Types who will try to rope you into cross-country running and mixed rugby and before the day is out, you can bet that Olivia Organiser will be urging you to take your turn at manning the second-hand bookstall/watering the Swiss cheese plant/filling the Aid to Everywhere in the World collecting box. Smile, be friendly, be pleasant to them all. If only one turns out to be a future friend, you will have had a very good first day.

It is very tempting for the first few weeks in a strange place to spend all your free time on the telephone to your friends back in your old home town, or stretched out on the bed writing pages and pages of frantic letters. But try to get involved in some activities – if you went to ballet classes before, get your parents to help you track down a dancing school near your new home. If horse riding is your thing, scan the *Yellow Pages* for stables and ask at school if anyone else goes riding. That way you widen your circle of potential friends and begin to feel more at home.

## Chapter 4

# Pouring Oil On Troubled Waters

*"There are three sides to every question; your side, his side and to hell with it."*
(Anon 20th century)

No matter how great your friendship is, it will have its stormy patches. Every relationship does. Conflict is part of everyday life and not all of it need be A Bad Thing.

Having a row doesn't mean that you will never be friends with the other person again. What it does mean is that one of you might have to make the first move in patching things up. And to do that you need to work out why you were fighting in the first place.

## WHY DO FRIENDS FIGHT?

1. Because they try to change each other's opinions.
2. Because they like to be the centre of attention.
3. Because they simply feel in the mood for a good argument.
4. Because they want to blame someone else for something that has gone wrong for them.

## HOW DO THEY FIGHT?

Different people have different ways of expressing annoyance or anger. Take a look at these types.

*BELINDA THE BICKERER*
Belinda never really has anything specific to fight about but she niggles away at little things, like "You should have told me you were going to wear a skirt – I'm in a T-shirt and leggings and you are all dressed up" and "You said that film was meant to be really good – it was rubbish." Now you weren't to know that Belinda was planning to wear leggings and you were only repeating what you had

heard about the film. But Belinda is self-conscious about not wearing the right thing and prefers to make it look like your fault. When she doesn't enjoy the film, she prefers to blame you rather than simply accept that everyone's tastes are different.

*How to handle Belinda:* Say "Just ring me any time you want to know what I am wearing" and "Next time, why don't you choose which film we see?"

## NATASHA THE NITPICKER

Natasha likes to argue over such tiny little issues that the rest of the world has difficulty spotting what the problem is. "You said you would phone back in 15 minutes and you've been 30." "It's not fair; you've sat next to the window for the last three mornings."

*How to handle Natasha:* It's hard. Let her sit by the window and within a week, she will be moaning that the draught is bothering her.

## STEVE THE SHOCKER

Steve says outrageous things to get attention and then argues when no-one believes him. This is the type to boast that he scored 15 goals in 17 minutes against Lower Throbbing Under 15s and then get furious and turn puce about the gills when someone points out that the final score was only 3-2. He will tell you that he isn't scared of anything – and then beat a hasty retreat when Mr Biggins of Biology brings in a grass snake. And he boasts about all his skills and talents – and flies off the handle if you say that you know someone who does it better.

*How to handle Steve:* Smile sweetly and say, "Oh yes, Steve – and the rest." Or simply smile and wander off. It's hard to argue when no-one's around to listen.

## STEPHANIE THE SULKER

You can't actually have a row as such with Stephanie because the moment she doesn't get her own way, she goes into a mega-decline. When someone disagrees with her opinion, she pouts, lowers her eyes, turns her back and sulks. Ask her what's wrong and she'll say "Nothing" in martyred tones; tell her that you will do what she wants and she will sigh and say, "No, it's all right, I don't really matter, do I?" She is trying to make you feel guilty for having a mind of your own. Don't let her.

*How to handle Stephanie:* Say "What production do you think we should do this term – *The Pied Piper* or *Grease?*" If she doesn't express an opinion, or she does but then sulks because the vote goes the other way, ignore her and get on with doing what you want. But make sure she doesn't have an excuse to sulk. Give her a chance to have her own way too – if you chose the video last Saturday night, let her choose one this time round.

## WENDY THE WHINGER

Go ice-skating and Wendy will moan that it's cold. Go for a walk in the woods and Wendy won't like the trees. Go shopping on Saturday and Wendy will say it is spoilt because of the crowds. She probably got her own way by whining as a kid and has never grown out of it.

*How to handle Wendy:* Ignore her.

*TABITHA TELL-TALE*
Tabitha loves dropping other people in it. She'll be the first to split when you spend your lunch money on a large Yorkie bar or get a detention for drawing faces of Snoopy on your headteacher's windscreen. When you tell her what you think of sneaks, she will start shouting and saying "Well, it's your own fault, you shouldn't have done it." Whether or not you should have done it is one thing; whether she should be a tell-tale is quite another.

*How to deal with Tabitha:* Next time she says "What are you doing tomorrow?", say, "Can't tell you, Tabs, you can't be trusted." See how she likes that one.

# WHAT SORTS OF SITUATION LEAD TO ROWS?

1. Never letting the other person get a word in edgeways. When they start to tell you about the problem they have with money, you say, "Oh, I know, and let me tell you about the time ... "

2. Always being late for everything. If you say you will meet outside the bowling alley at 5 o'clock you turn up at 5.30. You say "I'll phone back in half an hour," but it's at least two hours before you remember.

3. Always borrowing things – and usually forgetting to give them back.

4. Running down your friend's parents, brothers, grannies, black Labrador, tank of tropical fish. Kids can yell at their own families and criticise them till kingdom come, but let anyone from outside suggest that their dad's dress sense is abysmal or that their brother is a weed, and woe betide them.

5. Making fun of their religion or culture. This is the lowest thing to do. Don't ever jeer at someone because they wear different clothes or eat foods that you think are strange.

## RULES FOR GETTING THE BEST OUT OF A ROW

Even when you have a big bust-up, it is quite possible to turn the argument from being a negative thing into a positive thing.

### 1. *DON'T SUPPRESS – EXPRESS!*
If you think to yourself, "Oh no, we're having a row and that means the end of the world is at hand and I had better shut up," the row will probably stop. For now. But it will start again another day over some similar issue. Instead of suppressing your feelings, express them. But calmly. Say something like "I know you disagree with me, but on this issue I just can't change my mind," or "No, I can't lend you my new jacket – it's really important to me and it took me ages to save up for it. Ask me again in a

couple of months."

## 2. *STOP BEING PASSIVE – GET ACTIVE!*

Sometimes having an argument with a good friend can be like hurling yourself off the top diving board into a pool of melted ice. It gives you an almighty shock. Suddenly things you have taken for granted for 12 years don't seem quite so cut and dried. Could you be *wrong*? you ask yourself. Is it possible that Emily's idea is better than yours? When you start actively questioning instead of passively accepting, you develop into an even more thoroughly wonderful person than you were before.

## 3. *LEARN TO NEGOTIATE*

Find the bits of the argument that you do both agree on and then discuss the things that are making you angry with each other. Maybe you have both agreed to share a birthday party – but you want a fancy dress do and your friend wants a barbecue. How about a barbecue in fancy dress? Perhaps you are off to the cinema but can't agree on what film to see. Is one of them available on video – if so, why not hire that one and see the other? Or perhaps you could see one this week and the other one next week. Remember that there is a difference between an argument and a row – you can argue constructively, which is, after all, just what a debate is.

## 4. *DON'T MIX A SOUND ARGUMENT WITH INSULTS*

Don't use an argument as an excuse to say things you never meant to say and which you will regret later on, e.g.

"I hate your mother", "Everyone says you smell." It is very easy in the heat of a row to say things like "It wouldn't be safe to do that, you stupid old cow." What you are doing is giving a good reason why not to do something – because it would be unsafe – but the other person only hears the insult and reacts accordingly. She calls you a "slimy snake" and so it goes on.

## 5. *DON'T DRAG IN SIDE ISSUES*
Another easy trap to fall into. When you and Miranda are fighting over the fact that she has lost your roller pen, don't suddenly say, "And by the way, you were really horrid to my sister last week." That is not the point right now. Concentrate on sorting out one problem at one time.

## 6. *EXPLAIN YOUR VIEWPOINT*
When someone asks you why you feel cross, don't just say, "Because I do, so there." Tell them, quietly and calmly, the way you feel. If you know that certain situations always lead to arguments, think of ways of avoiding them. You may be very angry about something that is not even your friend's fault. You may have got hold of the wrong end of the stick. When you are ready to express yourself, go through the points and watch your friend's face – allow them to set the record straight if some of the things you say are wrong.

*What usually happens:* Jane always says she will meet you at the bus stop before you go into town but she is never on time. You end up missing the bus, hanging around in the cold and getting more and more angry.

*What not to do:* Say, "I'm not going into town with you because you are always late."

*The best plan:* The next time Jane says she will be at the bus stop at 10.30, say "Maybe we could meet in town – that way, if you are late, I can look round the shops."

*What usually happens:* You really like Laura but whenever you and she get together with a group of other friends, she jokes about all your shortcomings.

*What not to do:* Say, "Either we go around together or not at all – you're horrid when you are with other people."

*The best plan:* Say, "I'm sure you didn't mean it, but I felt really put down when you told everyone at the club about how clumsy I get when I am nervous."

*What usually happens:* Emma borrows your homework when she is stuck on hers – and when it turns out that some of your answers are wrong, she shouts at you for getting her a bad mark.

*What not to do:* Jump up and have a slanging match in the middle of class, saying, "You lying little cheat, Emma Soames, I hate you."

*The best plan:* The next time Emma asks to borrow your maths prep, say, "I don't think that's a good idea; after all, you know how often I make mistakes and I would hate for you to suffer on my account."

# HOW TO HANDLE A BUST-UP
(or Handy Hints for Keeping Cool When the Heat is On)
*"Be wiser than other people if you can but
do not tell them."*
(Lord Chesterfield)

## 1. *SAY WHAT YOU WANT*
It's no good saying, "I'm bored/we never do anything
interesting/you always do what you want" if you are not
prepared to come up with some better ideas.

## 2. *SAY HOW YOU FEEL*
If you feel angry, say so. If you feel let down, say in what
way. Keeping anger bottled up inside is destructive, but
hurling plates, smashing beakers and kicking the
neighbour's pet Persian is not particularly constructive
either. If you say what is bugging you, you give your
friend a chance to put it right.

## 3. *LISTEN TO WHAT THE OTHER PERSON WANTS*
It takes two people to make an argument. If your friend is
dead set on spending the afternoon making paper spiders
for her Hallowe'en party and you have no strong feelings
either way, give in. Even if making spiders is not high on
your list of fun things to do, and even if you think
Hallowe'en parties are a drag, you will be pleasing her
and she'll owe you a couple of favours for the future.

## 4. *DON'T BE A MARTYR*
Having listened to both sides of the argument, don't agree

for the sake of a quiet life. None of this "Oh, all right then, we'll do it your way. Don't worry about me – I don't mind," delivered in tones of abject misery. If you don't like the decision, say so, but say it nicely. "Count me out this time – maybe we can get together again next weekend."

## 5. *DON'T SHOUT*

If you shout in the middle of an argument, your voice goes higher and higher and squeakier and squeakier and then you start coughing because you've yelled so much and that makes you look silly. Say what you want to say firmly and clearly but without yelling. It's hard to do when you are feeling uptight but it is amazing how effective it is – even if only because the rest of them are so stunned that you are being quiet for once, that they are lost for words.

## 6. *NEVER SAY "YOU'RE WRONG" EVEN WHEN YOU THINK THEY ARE*

Say "That's one way of looking at it," or "I know that is how you do it, but it wouldn't work for me."

## 7. *IF YOU KNOW YOU WERE IN THE WRONG, SAY SO*

It's hard to do but people end up liking you for it. And you feel good when you've said, "Sorry, my mistake," or "I didn't mean to hurt you and I shouldn't have said what I did."

### 8. *REMEMBER THAT BEING THE FIRST TO APOLOGISE IS NOT A SIGN OF WEAKNESS*

It is a sign of maturity and strength. Even if you think you were in the right, say something like "I hate this atmosphere between us – can't we start again?"

# WAYS OF SOLVING ARGUMENTS

### 1. *THE CRACKDOWN*

"We do it my way – or not at all." Result – your friends resent you and they all beat a hasty retreat, leaving you with no option but to go it alone. Not a good plan.

### 2. *GIVING IN*

Sounds like the easy way out at the time, but the same argument will keep cropping up until you resolve it. Only next time, Theo will say, "Oh, but you didn't mind last week, so what's the problem this time?"

### 3. *AVOID THE ISSUE*

Change the subject, dash off to the loo, remember a forgotten piece of homework suddenly. This is sometimes an effective way of cooling down until everyone is in a better frame of mind to sort things out, but you can't go on avoiding things for ever and the longer you put it off, the more of a state you are likely to be in.

### 4. *COMPROMISE*

Sometimes it works, sometimes you end up doing what

no-one wants to do at all.

5. *RESOLUTION*
Set yourself a timescale – say half an hour at break time –
and say "Right, we'll get this sorted." That leaves little
time for slanging matches and accusations and means
that everyone knows where they stand as soon as
possible.

| RIGHT | WRONG |
|---|---|
| "Let's go home and sleep on it and try to sort something out tomorrow." | "Go on, admit it – you're stupid." |
| "Perhaps I got it wrong; say it again." | "Of course I'm right – any idiot can see that." |
| "Shall we ask the others what they think?" | "Everyone knows you're wrong." |

# FIVE FUN WAYS OF MAKING UP

1. Play "Consequences", writing down silly adjectives for
the people involved and making up fantasy endings of
what might have happened had you never made up.

2. Bake a friendship cake – you each put in the three
ingredients you like most. It sometimes tastes a little odd
but it usually works a treat. The best one I tasted had

mashed banana, chocolate chips and coconut (from Heidi) and cinnamon, raisins and apple (from Lauren).

3. If you think you might fight again, think up a Peace Password – you say "cotton socks" or "frilly knickers" or whatever to each other at the first sign of trouble. The more ludicrous the better – if you are laughing you can't be fighting.

4. If you've got the spare cash, go out and choose each other a pair of exotic dangly earrings or buy two magazines you have never read before and do all the quizzes on "How to Make Boys Adore You" and "How to Become a Teenage Star".

5. Give each other a big hug and a bigger bag of popcorn.

## ALL FRIENDS TOGETHER?

In an ideal world, everyone would get on famously with everyone else. But as we all know, life isn't like that. Sometimes you find you have two super friends, both of whom you really like and get on well with – and they cannot stand the sight of one another. So what do you do? Basically, not a lot. There is no reason why, if you like Anna and you like Pippa, you should not go on being friends with them both. If you are throwing a party, it won't matter if they don't get on because there will be plenty of other people around for them to mingle with.

Don't compromise your friendships by inviting one and not the other – it is up to each of them to decide whether or not they will attend if the other is going to be there. If you know that sparks fly every time they are together, invite them around to your house singly. Perhaps you could see Anna one weekend and Pippa the next. But whatever you do, don't let their personal animosities colour your friendship. Their hang-ups are their concern, not yours.

## BEWARE THE GREEN-EYED MONSTER!

*"Anybody can sympathise with the sufferings of a friend, but it requires a very fine nature to sympathise with a friend's success."*
(Oscar Wilde)

Sometimes it's not your warring friends you have to pacify – it's yourself! We all know that awful gnawing feeling inside when everything seems to be going right for everyone else – and not for us. We have all sat in class watching our best friend blush prettily as she accepts first place in the essay competition while we are twelfth yet again. "Well done," we have said and inside we have been screaming, "I wish it was me and not you getting all the praise and attention."

We all know about not coveting our neighbour's ox or ass – but sometimes it is pretty hard not to covet their dishy-looking boyfriend, their designer trainers or their forthcoming holiday in the Seychelles. When they are surrounded by admiring friends all ooh-ing and aah-ing over their latest triumph, it is all too easy to say to ourselves, "Oh well, I never did like her anyway."

But real friendship doesn't work like that. Real Friends can feel envious and jealous – but they don't let it get the upper hand. Look at it this way – when everything is going swimmingly for Amanda Jane and you feel cheesed off, remember that in a few weeks it could be you that keeps landing on your feet and Amanda who is having a down patch. Be good to her now and share her pleasures and she will do the same for you later on.

And what about those kids who always come top without really working at all, while you are sitting up half the night memorising the battles of the Civil War and writing essays on the glacial valleys of Scandinavia – and still getting B minus? Feeling jealous won't improve your marks – and the chances are that they are envying you because you can run 100 metres in point two of a second or perform a double back somersault with flip over the vaulting horse in the gym. In the end, the only person who suffers from jealousy is the person doing the envying – it doesn't get you anywhere, makes you frown a lot and is very exhausting.

*Chapter 5*

# BUT IF I DON'T, THEY WON'T LIKE ME ANY MORE

### (Handling peer group pressure)

From the day we are born, we crave approval. We want people to notice our achievements and praise our appearance. And we soon learn that life tends to run a little smoother when we have the approval of others.

Little kids want the approval of their parents first and foremost. They know that when they say, "Look, Mum, I can tie my shoelaces," or "I can write my name," they will be rewarded with smiles and congratulations and probably even a KitKat and a tube of Smarties.

Once you go to school, you learn that when the teachers approve of you, things go well and you get to be House Captain and when they don't, life becomes much more difficult and you spend a lot of time cleaning the athletics cups.

## Your Peers And Pressure

And then other people's opinions start mattering – sometimes even more than your parents' and teachers'. You start to want the unfailing approval of your friends, the kids of your own age whose ideas and views on everything from fashion to nuclear fallout probably differ fairly radically from those of your family. Suddenly it matters more whether Jamie likes your new hairstyle than whether your mum thinks you look like a scalped raccoon; and it becomes vitally more important that you get that pair of wicked lace-up ankle-boots than those slip-ons from Clarks that your mum thinks are so suitable.

It gets pretty confusing. At home there is one set of rules and with your friends there is another. Things that used to matter seem less important, and things that you never thought of before take on gargantuan proportions.

*What used to matter:* Having a hug from Mum and Dad and being told you were their best boy/girl.

*What matters now:* Getting the thumbs-up from Dave and Pete and being told that you are one cool dude.

*What used to matter:* Being good all week so Mum and Dad would take you out on Saturday.
*What matters now:* Being good all week so Mum and Dad say you don't have to go out with them on Saturday.

*What used to matter:* Impressing the teachers so you got to look after the class hamster at half-term.
*What matters now:* Impressing Boo and Kim so that they let you around with their gang at half-term.

*What used to matter:* Talking to Mum and Dad about sports day or your camping holiday in Wales.
*What matters now:* Talking to your friends about the meaning of life.

Being with your parents and being with your friends can sometimes seem like inhabiting two different planets. The things that matter most to Mum and Dad – "Have you finished your homework?", "Your bedroom looks like the town tip," and "Take that look off your face," are totally unimportant to your friends. But to your parents, the fact that you want to do what your friends do, wear what they wear and be seen where they think it is cool to be seen, is something they just don't understand. You don't want to hurt them, but you do want to be one of the crowd. They want to be Good Parents, but someone threw away the rule book. Confusing, isn't it?

*What your friends say to you:* Fancy going to the Zombie Metalheads concert on Saturday?

*What you say to your parents:* EVERYONE is going to the concert and I'll feel stupid if you say I can't go.

*What they say:* You are not going and that is that.

*What they mean:* We've read dreadful things about kids being given drugs to try and we are scared for you. If we don't let you go, you'll be safe.

*What your friends say to you:* Let's go for a moonlight swim.

*What you say to your parents:* All the gang were going and I didn't want to be left out.

*What they say:* Oh, and I suppose if they had all decided to hurl themselves off a cliff, you would have followed blindly on?

*What they mean:* I did that 20 years ago and caught pneumonia.

*What you friends say to you:* You're 14 and you don't drink? Go on, it won't hurt you.

*What you say to your parents:* It was only one glass of wine and Jenny said it wouldn't do any harm.

*What they say to you:* Oh, and Jenny is a world expert on alcoholism, is she?

*What they mean:* We love you, we worry ourselves sick, 14 is far too young to drink away from home and we don't know what to say to make you see we care.

*What your friends say:* Why do you have to be home by 10 pm?

*What you say to your parents:* Everyone else's parents lets them stay out till 11.30 pm.
*What they say:* Well, we're not everyone else's parents.
*What they mean:* I may be getting this wrong but I reckon that's too late, and on this one I am standing my ground.

Looking at the world around you just makes everything even more confusing.

• You switch on the television and there are all those sylph-like models strutting around in minuscule skirts, tossing their freshly-washed hair over their spotless shoulders and falling elegantly into the arms of some hunk in a pair of skin-tight jeans. In that world it seems as if having a 22-inch waist and no dandruff matters far more than a handful of GCSEs and the ability to name the capitals of Europe.

• Your mum's a French teacher, your dad is a chartered accountant and they have great hopes that you will go to university and follow a "worthwhile career". But all they ever seem to do is work, eat and sleep, and their idea of a fun night is watching *Panorama* on the television. Their world seems dull – is all the hard work worth it?

• Your friend Rosanna is 15 and looks 18. She goes into pubs and nightclubs and tells you all about the great guys who chat her up and the wonderful times she has. You know your mum would have a fit if you looked and acted like her, but her world seems much more exciting than yours. Rosanna says live a little, your mum says don't you dare. Who's right?

In your sane moments (and everyone has them between those mad sessions with the lilac hair dye and the head-on argument with their mother over the fact that their little brother, who should have been consigned to the refuse collection department years ago, has been at your Seaweed and Compost Face Mask and used it as finger paint) – you know what is *right*, what is *pretty risky* and what is definitely *wrong*.

When it comes to turning down Crazy Cathy's invitation to daub the school canteen with graffiti or Dimbo Derek's plan to blow up the chemistry lab, you have no qualms about saying no. But it's all those other "shall I, shan't I?" situations which can cause a whole heap of heartache and indecision.

## NO! – THE HARDEST WORD IN THE ENGLISH LANGUAGE

Saying "No, I can't do that" and meaning it is a very, very hard thing to do. While you can say no to someone you dislike who is doing something stupid, everyone worries about saying No to people they care about.

## WHY DO WE WORRY ABOUT SAYING NO?

### 1. *WE THINK THAT OUR FRIENDS WILL STOP LIKING US*

"If I don't do what Lisa wants, she won't be my friend."
Possible. If so, she wasn't worth having as a friend in the
first place. People who only like you while they are
getting their own way haven't grown up, don't care about
anyone except themselves and are probably only using
you as the means to an end.

### 2. *IT MAKES US FEEL GUILTY*

"I can't say I won't do Sally's homework for her – she
looks so miserable when I say no." Sally has obviously
discovered how to make you feel guilty and is using it to
full advantage. The thing is, we are all taught that it is A
Good Thing to:

(a) be nice to people
(b) think of others before ourselves
(c) do unto others as you would wish others to do unto
you
(d) etc etc etc.

When we even consider going against one of these
Moral Maxims, we feel horribly guilty. Now these are very
worthy sentiments and awfully good for writing in
people's autograph books, but like all Good Ideas they
work some of the time. Think about why you don't want
to do Sally's homework.

(a) By the time you have done your own, you won't have
time.
(b) You are finding it hard yourself and will only make

107

mistakes which she will get into trouble for.

(c) You have done it eight times this term already and want to say, "Give me a break."

So what's wrong with any of those? That's the truth, you've thought it through and none of those excuses are hurting anyone. *So don't feel guilty.*

### 3. *WE IMAGINE THAT IF WE SAY NO THIS TIME, NO-ONE WILL ASK US AGAIN*

"If I say I don't want to go swimming with the gang, they might not include me in any more of their activities."

Why don't you want to go swimming?

(a) I can't swim.

(b) I haven't got a swimsuit that fits and I'm too hard up to buy a new one this week.

(c) I know someone will duck me and I hate having my head under water.

(d) I've already arranged to go out with my parents that day.

See? Perfectly good reasons. So tell them. If you don't want to admit to being scared of water, prime the parents and use the last excuse. (An allergy to chlorinated water is a pretty nifty let-out as well.) And add something like "But how about we all get together next weekend and go to the Karaoke?"

### 4. *WE REMEMBER GETTING INTO TROUBLE FOR SAYING NO AS LITTLE KIDS*

When you are trying hard to win someone's approval, your little old subconscious mind works overtime. It remembers that when you screeched "No! No! No! Go Away Smelly Old Granny!" when you were two and a quarter and a little bit, your mother said, "Don't you ever let me hear you speaking to your grandmother like that again." She didn't approve. And when you were six and your father sent you to bed, you yelled, "No! No! Shan't! Won't! Piggy Daddy!" and he stopped your pocket money, hid your Lego and refused to take you to the swings for three whole days. He didn't approve.

And your subconscious mind, which stores up all sorts of useful information, like fire burns you, and six Mars Bars make you sick, and making tea for your mother for a week immediately prior to your birthday is a good idea, remembers the times when saying No was not the brightest idea you ever had.

But you are not two and a quarter and a little bit any more and you are no longer six either. You are now old enough to say No nicely. And that is the difference.

5. *EVERYONE ELSE IS SAYING YES*
It is very easy to follow the crowd and agree for the sake of peace and quiet. But funnily enough, after a while, people start thinking you are wet for having no opinions of your own. If you disagree, say so. And say why.


## HOW TO SAY NO

1. Always put the actual word "No" first. "No, I'm sorry, I can't come over tonight." "No, I don't like that idea." "No,

locking Gloria in the garage would be a mean thing to do."

2. Don't back down. If you say, "No, I don't want to pinch a chocolate bar from the cafeteria" and then say, "Oh, all right then" because everyone else is giving it a go, no-one will believe you next time. If you find it hard, say your "No" calmly and firmly and then walk away. If your "friends" are constantly trying to get you to do things you believe are wrong, talk to your mum or dad or teacher about it.

3. Don't feel guilty. If you say no to something that doesn't feel right for you, you have no cause to feel guilty. If you say yes, when inside your head you are screaming no, you do have cause to feel guilty. You have let yourself down.

## PEOPLE IT'S VERY HARD TO SAY NO TO

Sometimes, we become so infatuated with someone that we really cannot see anything wrong in them. To us, everything they say, believe and do is amazing. We copy their hairstyle, their speech, even the way they sneeze, in order to be like them. Never mind *Star Trek* and *The Clones from Planet Coz*, we become the experts in imitation.

Your parents will probably notice and say something along the lines of: "Haven't you got an original brain cell in your head?", "Oh, look, here comes Annie Mark 2," or "That new hairstyle makes you look like an infuriated hedgehog."

To be honest, all that is pretty harmless. If you want to go round being like someone else, that's fine. But putting people way up on a pedestal does have its dangers – for them and for you. There is no way they can go on being the perfect person you imagine them to be – no-one is. And one day, when Angel Annie starts losing her halo, you might have to think again.

## SIGNS THAT YOUR FRIEND'S HALO IS BEGINNING TO WOBBLE

1. Gemma is always doing things and saying to you, "Promise you won't tell." Ask yourself whether some of the things you are being asked to keep quiet about are perfectly legal, perfectly safe and perfectly honest. If the answer is no, think long and hard about having too much to do with her.

2. Ben is always roping you into scams that upset other people, thinking up practical jokes which leave other friends upset or embarrassed, and then saying it was your idea. Ask yourself how you would feel if you were on the receiving end. If you don't like the idea, it's time to think it out again.

3. Debbie cheats a lot. Copying someone else's homework with their permission once in a while is one thing; snooping in the teacher's folder for the answers to a half-

term test is another. If she can cheat on schoolmates and teachers, one day you can bet she will cheat on you.

Sometimes you will be asked to do things "because you're my friend". But friendship should never be a reason for doing something that you are not happy about.

*SUSAN'S STORY*
Susan was horrified when she saw her friend Natalie pick up a scarf from a shop counter and slip it into her bag. When she challenged her, she said it was for her grandma's birthday and it was the only way she could get her a present. "It's dead easy," Natalie told Susan, "Try it – go on, pinch those black earrings." Susan had the good sense to walk away there and then.

"Inside, I didn't know what to do," said Susan. "I knew I could never steal myself, but Natalie said that if I told anyone about what she had done, she'd see I suffered for it, and I think she meant it. And I knew her mum had just lost her job and I thought it would add to their problems. In the end I kept quiet, but I didn't hang around with her any more. Last month I heard she had been caught stealing magazines from the local newsagent."

Natalie was the loser in the end. Not only was she indulging in crime, but she lost someone who could have been a really good and reliable friend.

*TARA'S STORY*
Some situations are more difficult.

Tara had been friends with Becky since they were at

primary school but when they were both 13, Becky
started calling Tara a wimp and a baby because she didn't
want to try cigarettes or alcohol. "In the end, Becky gave
up on me and I suddenly had nothing to do at weekends,"
said Tara. "I felt very lonely so one weekend I phoned her
and said my mum and dad were out and did she want to
come over for drinks. She came and we drank lots of wine
from my dad's drinks cupboard. Of course, we were both
ill, Dad found out and I got into awful trouble. I was
grounded for a month but I thought Becky would really
like me for being cool. In fact, she didn't take any more
notice of me than before. All that happened was that I lost
my parents' respect and it took ages to rebuild their
trust."

Tara lost her parents' goodwill and she was really ill,
and all because she wanted to impress someone who just
wasn't worth it.


## WHEN THE RISKS JUST AREN'T WORTH THE HASSLE

While you are growing up, you get lots of advice along the
lines of "Be careful", "Stop and think" and "Don't take
unnecessary chances." All very sound pieces of advice –
but whatever your parents may tell you, taking a few risks
and chances is a normal party of growing up. If you never
risked failing, you would never succeed. If you never
risked losing, you could never win. And if you never
risked being hurt, you would never make a friend in the

first place.

But there are risks and risks, and some are just not worth taking. A chap called Roger Owen, who has spent a lot of time writing about growing up, says that you should "Be a thermostat, not a thermometer." Sounds a bit technical but if you think about it, a thermostat controls the environment around it and a thermometer is controlled by the temperature outside. If you let your mates tell you what to do, where to go, what to drink and whether to smash windows, you are just a passive thermometer. Saying No to the things that make you feel uneasy makes you an active thermostat.

## WHEN YOU'RE DOING SOMETHING VERY WRONG

Paul was in a gang, but there's a difference between a group of kids going around together and having a good time, and a group of kids going around looking for trouble and giving other people a hard time.

"I went around with this group of guys, mainly for the skateboarding. Then one day on the way home, one of them started daring the rest of us to drop things down from the motorway bridge onto cars below. I'm quite small and one of the big guys grabbed hold of me, put a stone in my hand and told me to throw it or else. I'm ashamed to say I did but I made sure it went on the hard shoulder. Then I ran home. I was really scared and told my dad and he said I should give that crowd a wide berth in future. I did, but it wasn't easy because they teased me all the time at school and called me chicken. Luckily I joined up with some other guys from the football club and now I go around with them."

## SMOKING

You would think that by the time a kid was old enough to lace up their own Doc Martens and find their way to the chip shop, they would have sussed the fact that cigarettes can kill you. What's more, your cigarettes can kill other people. But like most things, it's a new experience, and lots of teenagers think they look grown-up smoking. If you don't want to smoke, say so. Something like "No thanks, I want to live long enough to make my millions." Some kids smoke because they think it looks cool – meanwhile it is making the inside of their lungs look like the bottom of Granny's grate, ageing their skin, making their hair smell, staining their fingers and giving them breath like a power station smoke stack. Your friends will come up with all sorts of reasons why you should smoke.

*Myth:* Smoking will relax you for the party.
*Fact:* Smoking will send your blood pressure soaring, your heart racing, and any kick you feel is because you are becoming addicted.

*Myth:* Smoking will help you slim.
*Fact:* There is a grain of truth in this because smoking speeds up your metabolic rate, so you burn calories

faster. It's only temporary – when you have the good sense to quit, you will put the weight back on and find it harder to lose. And don't think, OK then, I will carry on puffing – after all, who wants to be thin and dead?

*Myth:* Everyone does it.
*Fact:* Oh no, they don't. More and more people are giving up smoking every year. Smokers are in the minority and you have only to look around a restaurant to see the filthy looks puffers get from the rest of us.

*Myth:* I can stop any time I like.
*Fact:* The longer you smoke, the harder it gets to give up. It's better not to start. If you have started, stop right now. You need the next 70 years to make your mark on the world.

## DRINKING

It's pretty hard to go to a party where people are offering you lager and cider and wine and say, "No thanks, I'll have an orange juice." So lots of kids say, "OK, just one glass" and then, when that one's finished, "Just one more." Then they spend several hours forming a close relationship with the inside of the nearest loo.

*Fact:* Alcohol is a drug. What's more, it zooms straight into your bloodstream, unlike crisps, sausages on sticks and pizza fingers. It has a rapid effect on the brain, making you feel less uptight and rather floaty. Great, you cry! Not so great. It makes you take risks that you wouldn't even contemplate when you were stone cold sober.

*Fact:* Alcohol intensifies your emotions. So if you started off moderately happy, it may make you giggly and soppy for a while, and then wham! the effect wears off and you feel ghastly, let down, miserable and angry. And if you felt a bit low when you started, look out Doomsville. You will feel so weepy and miserable that you will wonder why you bothered.

*Fact:* Alcohol is fattening. All those calories it contains do nothing except fly with the speed of light to your hips.

*Fact:* Too much alcohol makes you sick. Boys in particular seem to think it is very Jack-the-laddish to quaff away at cans of lager and beer. They seem to think that rolling around under the effects of drink is macho. It's not. It's pathetic and if they are doing it to impress girls, they should know that any girl with a quarter of a grain of common sense will run a mile. What's more, if you pass out and are sick, you could choke and die. And then it's a bit late to say "Whoops".

The best way to get to know alcohol as you grow up is to have an At Home Only policy. Get your parents to let you have the odd glass of wine at Sunday lunch if that is what they drink – or a little cider or whatever else is the custom. See how it make you feel. Then, by the time you are 18 you will at least know what you can and can't manage. If your parents are teetotallers, talk the whole issue over with them. Explain that you feel that you need to know what it tastes like and the effect it has on you. Better the devil you know than the devil you don't. In the meantime, say no. You wouldn't think twice about refusing a plate of tripe and onions if you didn't like it, or turning down a slice of mouldy bread. So just say, "No thanks, I can't stand the taste" and pour yourself a Pepsi.

## DRUGS

Considering you are intelligent enough to have got this far in the book, I assume you are not crazy enough to get caught up in the illegal substances scene. If anyone, ever, anywhere, offers you anything at all suspect, say no and then get the hell out of there. Don't even stop to consider. And tell someone. You could save some other kid's life. And if you are still tempted, remember this:

1. You have only got one body and it has to last a lifetime.

2. Drugs mess you up emotionally, make it harder to do well at school and lower your stamina levels.

3. Drugs are illegal and could land you in big trouble with the law.

4. Drugs don't solve problems, they create them. However miserable or confused or lost you feel, taking drugs won't cure you. You have probably heard about Ecstasy, the newest "cult" drug on the teen scene. You may hear that it makes you feel great. It can also kill you. It certainly won't make your life better. If you feel a mess, ask an adult for help and stay alive to enjoy the next 70 years. Well, that's all been a bit heavy, hasn't it? Reading that lot you would think that nicotine addicts and alcohol addicts and drug pushers were waiting for you at every party. Not so. But you need to be aware that the risks are there. Once you know about them, you can say a firm No and get on enjoying life with your friends. And 99.9 per cent of kids you meet will be doing just the same thing.

## So How Good Are You At Saying No?

1. Philip produces a can of something odd and says that if you sniff it you will feel great. He says that all the kids with guts are doing it. Do you say:
(a) "OK"?
(b) "No way – I'm too young to die – and anyway, I respect my guts"?
(c) "Well, not now, because I'm in a bit of a rush, but maybe another day"?

2. Leanne's older brother who is only 16 says he's got the keys to a friend's car and why don't you go for a spin? Do you say:

(a) "No thanks" and tell someone pretty fast?
(b) "Well, just a little way, then"?
(c) "I can't, I've got to get home to feed the goldfish"?

3. Kelly says you can be in her gang but you have to smoke three cigarettes first. Do you say:
(a) "OK" and throw up behind the bus shelter?
(b) "Sorry, I'm saving my lungs for something worthwhile"?
(c) "Oh sorry, I thought this was a cool gang, not a load of ninnies – I'll give it a miss after all"?

*ANSWERS*
1. (a) Don't be insane. Sniffing substances is not just mildly risky. It is DOWNRIGHT DANGEROUS. Do it and you could be dead in a week.

(b) Great – reminds Philip of just how crazy he is and makes him think – even if he doesn't admit it.

(c) Feeble excuse. If you believe it is wrong, say so. Otherwise he will keep pestering you.

2. (a) Spot on. And this isn't telling tales – it is acting to prevent possible deaths – his, his passengers and other innocent drivers and passers-by.

(b) It only takes five seconds to kill someone.

(c) More feeble excuses.

3. (a) Why? Do you like cigarettes? No? Then say so. Would you eat rancid meat if someone told you to?

(b) Clever. Amusing, witty and very much to the point.

(c) Cleverer still. It lets them know that their gang is not as important as your health – and it just might (though I wouldn't bank on it) make them think about the consequences of puffing.

## Chapter 6

# ME AND MY SHADOW

*"I don't need a friend who changes when I change, and who nods when I nod: my shadow does that much better."*
**(Plutarch)**

All too often, you hear your parents moan, "That Amanda Jane is a bad influence on you," and just occasionally, "I think Louise is having a good effect on you." But of course our friends do influence the way we look, how we behave and how we view the world at large. This is great – as long as you don't copy them at the expense of your own individuality.

## EVERYBODY'S DIFFERENT

One thing is certain – when it comes to the fashion stakes, friends have a greater input than anyone else in our lives.

### UNIFORMLY SPLENDID

Oscar Wilde, who was prone to make the odd pertinent comment about most things, said of fashion: "It is a form of ugliness so intolerable that we have to alter it every six months."

That's probably going a bit far, but it is true that fashions come and fashions go, and the one thing that is certain is that the outfit splashed across the centre pages of *Just 17* this month is not going to look great on everybody. One season's shades of buttermilk and sludge may do nothing for you except make you look like a jaundiced pumpkin, while the next year's colours of caramel and coffee could turn you into a walking masterpiece.

1. FACT: What looks terrific on your friend Melanie may look daft on you. Take a look around any town centre shopping mall on a Saturday morning and treat yourself

to a good giggle. Take two 14-year-olds: one is five foot nothing, a bit on the plump side with shoulder-length blonde hair and beautiful fair skin. The other is skinny, five foot seven and growing, with short cropped ginger hair and acne. Yet both are dressed in lime green and purple miniskirts and cropped cardigans because Street Cred Sasha of Super Teen Magazine told them to. One looks like an over-ripe kiwi fruit and the other like a stick of seaside rock – and neither does themselves any credit.

2. FACT: Being a Copycat Clothes Horse isn't worth the cash. You may think your best friend looks like a million dollars in skin-tight denim jeans and a black body, and she probably does. But if you have a big bottom and over-active boobs you would look much better in long, floaty skirts and over-the-hip loose jackets. It doesn't matter one bit whether your hips are 32 inches or 38 inches – it's how you show them off (or don't) that counts in the style stakes. The layered look can do wonders for some girls – others look like a table that escaped from a downmarket jumble sale.

3. FACT: The chances of your parents approving of the way you and your friends dress are pretty slim. One of the reasons parents say things like "That's not a skirt, it's a pelmet," and "Shall I mend the tear in your blue jeans before you go out, dear?" is because they are worrying themselves silly over what their friends will think of your appearance. They imagine the gossip at the golf club: "How can Douglas let his daughter go around looking like

that?" They worry about whispers over the supermarket trolleys: "If that Hamish was my son, he would have that stud out of his nose as fast as you could say punk." Well, you may say, that is their problem. Your friends don't think any the worse of you because your mother wears trousers with elasticised waistbands or green eye shadow plastered on with a cake slice, even if you are mortified beyond belief, so why should they bother about your appearance? Then stop and ask yourself how many times you've said things like "Mum, when Fiona comes round, you will stop Dad telling silly jokes/clicking his teeth/ wearing that orange kipper tie, won't you?"

The best compromise is to agree that for family gatherings you will tone it down a bit – provided, of course, your father ditches the purple golf sweater with the natty little clubs embroidered around the cuffs.

4. FACT: Most kids want to look older than they really are. Some are lucky – they look grown-up when they are still at primary school. Others can reach the Sixth Form and still look about 12. And anyway, no-one is ever satisfied.

Getting together with friends to experiment with make-up is one of the best ways known of passing a wet weekend. Borrowing each other's eye shadows and lip gloss can create a whole host of new looks and give you the opportunity of finding out what doesn't suit you. The truth is that the best sort of make-up is the kind that doesn't look as if it is on; plastering black eyeliner and pillar-box red lipstick on your face makes you look like a painted doll, not a person.

Here again, copying for the sake of it can have disastrous results. Take the case of Natalie, who wanted a hairstyle just like her friend Margaret.

"Margaret has this brilliant bob – it looks great, just like the ads on TV. Her sister Elaine, who is training to be a hairdresser, did it, and I persuaded her to do it on me. But it looks horrendous. My hair is fine and wispy and it just lies against my head and I look gross."

Making the most of your best assets is the secret to looking good – not just being a mirror image of her next door.

## CARROTS, CELERY AND NO-CAL COLA

Your friend Beth may be one of those irritatingly lucky souls who can eat five jam doughnuts, half a packet of chocolate digestives and a quarter of a pound of cream caramels and still look like a reed. On the other hand, your friend Charlotte may well pick at her food, hate sweets and ice-cream and still be in line for understudy to the Roly Polys. That's metabolism for you. Rotten, unfair, grotty – but there it is.

But what happens when Charlotte decides that come what may, she is going to look like Beth? She stops eating. She lives on celery sticks and diet drinks. She gets thin. She also gets pale, her hair gets brittle, she has dark lines under her eyes and she eventually becomes ill. Thin she may be – happy she is not. If you want to lose weight, do it sensibly. Join up with like-minded friends, talk to your parents, see the doctor if necessary. But remember that between the ages of ten and 15 your body is driving itself into a frenzy coping with puberty, school, assimilation of new information, active sports – and it needs some fuel to do it on. Watch your weight – but never make a fetish out of it. No shape on earth is worth making yourself ill for.

# FRIENDLY INFLUENCES

As the above examples show, you shouldn't be a copycat. But friends can be a great influence on the way you look at things. Because they have different views, they can make you look at things you've never noticed, or have just taken for granted, in a different – often better – light.

## I NEVER KNEW THAT

It's a funny thing that when we look at ourselves, we always seem to see the bad bits first. Luckily for us, when our friends look at us, they see the good bits first. Try this test. Give your friend a piece of paper numbered one to six and ask him or her to write down six things about you. At the same time, take a piece yourself and write down six things about yourself. I bet that you will write more criticisms of yourself than your friend will. Look at this:

JANE                          JANE'S FRIEND
1. I am too fat                1. She's hilariously funny

127

| | |
|---|---|
| 2. I've got a good sense of humour | 2. She's a good listener |
| 3. I'm terrible at sport | 3. She's very good at French |
| 4. I am very forgetful | 4. She's always so enthusiastic and full of fun |
| 5. I am good at languages | 5. She can be a bit forgetful |
| 6. My front teeth are wonky | 6. She's a brilliant actress |

Jane didn't mention being good at acting and Jane's friend never thought of Jane as being "terrible at sport". Jane's friend didn't mention Jane's teeth or shape once – but she did say Jane was a good listener and full of fun.

As you grow up you realise that, if your friends have a good opinion of you, then maybe you should be kinder to yourself. Having friends is very good for your self-image.


## I SUPPOSE THEY'RE NOT ALL THAT BAD, REALLY

Somewhere between the ages of ten and 12, your parents stop being thoroughly wonderful, utterly caring, brilliantly witty and amazingly clever and become extremely irritating, determined to make your life difficult, embarrassing to take out in public and really rather stupid for their age. Of course, they haven't changed at all: but your perception of them has. And your friends can influence the way you look at parents.

*What your friends say:* "Does your Mum always call you tweety-pie?"
*What you think:* "Yes – I'm so used to it I don't notice but she had better stop right now or I'll be a laughing stock"

*What your friends say:* "We never have our meals in front of the television in our house."
*What you think:* "I must ask Mum to get out the best china and lay up the table when Erica comes for supper."

*What your friends say:* "Your dad's a real laugh."
*What you think:* "What – my dad? With his old jokes and belly laugh? I've always thought he was embarrassing. Maybe he can be quite funny at times."

*What your friends say:* "It must be great to have an older brother."
*What you think:* "For a fee, I can hire him out to you for a week – then see what you think."

*What your friends say:* "Your baby sister is cute."
*What you think:* "Not at three in the morning, she isn't – and not when she's torn up my maths homework. But then, come to think of it, she can be quite sweet – when she's cuddly or asleep."

*What your friends say:* "Your mum's a brilliant cook, isn't she? The food at your place is great."
*What you think:* "Is it? Well, I suppose she isn't bad, really. I suppose I've never thought about it."

129

# WHY DO YOU DO THAT?

Another thing about having friends who are different from you is that they let you look at the world in a new way. Friends from other countries may eat different foods, have different religions or believe in different ways of doing things. That doesn't mean your way is right or wrong, better or worse. Just different.

Tim made friends with Wang Le, a Chinese boy from Hong Kong who was at his school for a year while his parents were working in London. As a result, Tim tasted Chinese food for the first time, learnt a few words of Cantonese, went to a Chinese New Year party at Wang Le's house and is now saving all he can in order to visit him one day in Hong Kong.

Vanessa was friends with May, a Jamaican girl whose family lived next door. May invited Vanessa along to her Gospel Church youth club and although Vanessa still went to her own church on Sundays, she joined in some of the club activities and learnt gospel singing. Now May and Vanessa are singing a duet at the local music festival.

Friends can influence your thoughts on all sorts of things. You may never have given much thought to saving whales or banning fox-hunting – but if you become friends with someone who is keen on issues like that, you learn a lot about them, even if you end up disagreeing.

## Chapter 7

# MOVING ON – I REALLY LIKE YOU BUT ...

*I'm sorry you are wiser*
*I'm sorry you are taller,*
*I liked you better foolish*
*And I liked you better smaller.*
(Aline Kilmer)

Nothing stays the same for ever, and that includes friendship. Think about it.

When you were eight, you had straight hair, liked Wet Wet Wet, thought a good time was a trip to the zoo, and believed that the best food on earth was burger, chips and a double chocolate milkshake. Four years on, you have an acid perm, are into Heavy Metal, think zoos are the cruellest places on earth – and still go for burger, chips and a double chocolate milkshake!

Sometimes it can be like that with friends. Some last a lifetime, others seem to drift away in a couple of years. The person you idolised at 12 probably drives you crazy at 14, and your best pal at primary school may well have little in common with you by the second year at secondary school. It's not your fault and it's not their fault. It's called growing up.

Between the ages of 11 and 15 a lot of things change.

• You discover new hobbies and interests. People mature at different rates, and this is especially true during your teens, when you are growing up and maturing. You all get there in the end, but not at the same speed.

• You spend less time with the friends your parents chose for you and more time with friends of your own choice.

• You start to look ahead and think about what you want to do with your life.

• You start to question things that you used to take for granted.

• You experiment with new looks, new ideas and new people. The more people you meet, the greater the choice of friends you have. So it figures that when you leave your village school for a large secondary school, you are likely to find lots of people who share your interests.

So what do you do when you find the friend you had last year just doesn't interest you any more? It's not easy – people have feelings and it is easy to hurt them without meaning to.

## HOW TO HANDLE THE HANGERS-ON

*CLINGY CASSANDRA*
She clings like a limpet. "But you're my friend," she will say when you mention that you cannot go to her house every Sunday any more. She will wait for you outside school, offer you sweets and magazines – anything to keep you talking.

*What not to say:*
• "Oh, get lost, I'm bored with you."
• "You're so immature – it won't do my street cred any good to be seen hanging around with you."
• "I can't imagine what I ever saw in you."

*What you can say:*
• "I know we always used to go out on Sundays but I seem to be so busy these days – why don't we meet up on the

133

first Saturday of each month?"
• "I have to practise my tennis on Fridays if I want to make the team. But I'm sure Yvonne would like to go bowling with you."

*TUNNEL VISION TIM*
Because you and Tim have always enjoyed cricket, he expects you to spend every summer evening hitting sixes with him – and then on Saturday he wants to watch the Test Match with you. It's his only real interest and he cannot bear to think that you might have other things to do besides discuss Atherton's prowess or the fate of the one-day test against New Zealand.

*What not to say:*
• "Oh, go and stick your stumps somewhere else, can't you?"
• "You are so narrow-minded."
• "You're not even good at cricket."

*What you can say:*
• "I do enjoy our games of cricket, but I am getting quite keen on cycling and woodwork too. How about playing on Friday evenings?"
• "I know Wayne and Steve want to improve their bowling – why don't you play with them sometimes?"

*HELPLESS HARRIET*
She honestly believes that without you to lean on, her life will come to a rapid and messy end. "But who will help

me with my English project?" "But you always sit next to me on the bus," she will sob.

*What not to say:*
• "You are a prize-winning wimp."
• "It's time you stood on your own two flat feet."
• "I'm just too sophisticated for you these days."

*What you can say:*
• "You are much better at English than you think – you will do just fine."
• "Why don't you ask that new girl Ella to sit with you?"

*SAINTLY SHONA*
She's even harder to deal with. Ever since she took you under her wing when you were a new girl in town, she has been there to lend you money for your library fine, ring you up to remind you that your maths assignment is due in on Tuesday, or explain to you just why you haven't been chosen as Form Captain this term (usually because she has). She chose to act as your guardian angel long after you needed all that protection – because she needs to feel wanted. Now you don't need her constant chaperoning – but don't expect her to believe that. She will continue to telephone you at hourly intervals to make sure that your cold hasn't turned to flu/that your cat has had her kittens/that you have seen sense over your passion for Jack in the fifth form. She will also send you cards saying "Hugs and kisses from your bestest friend."

*What not to say:*
- "You are so sickly you make me want to puke."
- "Find someone else to nanny."
- "Yes, I am fine – or I was till you turned up."

*What you could say:*
- "I honestly think you should spend more time with Anthea – she needs someone sensible like you to lean on."
- "Oh listen, I can hear someone sobbing in distress in the gym. Why don't you go and take a look?"
- "I hear they want someone to form a help group for injured sparrows."

### MALICIOUS MELISSA

Melissa wants to be your friend, but if she can't be, she is going to make pretty sure that no-one else is either. She will get into a huddle with other kids, telling them all about your faults and failings and warning them of the dangers of being your friend.

*What not to say:*
- "Well, I could tell them a thing or two about you, so there."
- "All right then, you can still be my friend."
- "You're a beastly, lying, flat-footed moo."

*What you could say:*
- "You ought to be an author with your imagination."
- "You can be really nice when you are not being really horrible."

• "So I did make the right decision after all."

The great thing to remember is always to put yourself in the other person's position. If your friend doesn't have any other friends, try to help him or her make some more (that's why it is a good idea to suggest other kids who might be grateful for help). Think about why you want to drop this friend – is it because you really don't like them any more or because you have suddenly acquired new friends and new interests? Or could it be because no-one else likes them much and you think that their unpopularity might affect people's attitude to you? If so, is this really a good reason for dropping someone? Are you sure there is no place for her in your life? Whatever the reason and whatever you do, don't go around running her down or complaining about her to all and sundry.

## WHEN THE BOOT IS ON THE OTHER FOOT

Sometimes you will be on the receiving end. It will be you that is being dumped. It can hurt a lot to discover that your friend Louise finds the company of Juliet or Laura more scintillating than yours.

It is very tempting to blame yourself for being dumped. "I must be a horrid person if Louise doesn't want to be my friend any more," you think. "Perhaps if I had given her a better birthday present, she would still like me."

And when you have finished blaming yourself, you start

137

to feel angry. "How dare she treat me like that? Who does she think she is anyway?"

Anger is a natural reaction to that feeling we all dread – the feeling of rejection. We all want to be loved, admired and respected and when someone drops us, we feel discarded, second-rate and unwanted. When we feel cross, it is all too easy to lash out and say things we regret later on. What we need to do is take a couple of very deep breaths, think honestly about whether we have done anything really horrid and if not, make the best of it.

*WHAT NOT TO DO*
• Sob, wail and gnash your teeth.
• Call her names because she says that she can't make it to table tennis this week.
• Say "Well, I never liked you anyway."
• Sit up all night crying your eyes out and asking yourself what you did wrong. Chances are you did nothing wrong – you just outgrew one another.
• Phone her every evening, begging her to be your friend and bribing her with offers of your Sony Walkman for a month or a loan of your Lisa Stansfield video.
• Hang around being generally irritating.
• Don't think that you are horrible and that no-one will like you ever again, just because one person doesn't. Tell yourself it is her loss, not yours – or try to, anyway.

*WHAT TO DO*
• Tell her you hope she has a great time at the party/tap dance class/football match – and try to mean it.

- Find other friends.
- Still remember to send her a card on her birthday –
a good way of showing you still care.
- Be there when Juliet and Laura go off to see *The Scourge of the Alien Clunkheads* without Louise and she feels all rejected.

# I CAN'T COME OUT WITH YOU – I'M IN LOVE

The first time a boy asks you out – even if it only means sharing your peanut butter sandwiches and Twirl at lunch time – it's like the rest of the world vanishes in a sort of misty haze. You can't think of anything except HIM. You want to spend every free moment in his company and all your other friends seem to pale into insignificance beside him.

It's easy to say that you won't go to the cinema this week because *he* might phone or you will cancel your plans to go skating with Emma and Tony because the new love doesn't like ice. But if you want your friends to still be around when this fleeting romance is over, don't shut them out now. You can have boyfriends and girlfriends, old friends and new ones. They are not mutually exclusive.

Cutting yourself off from long-standing friends just because you have met someone who makes you go weak at the knees is one of the biggest mistakes boys and girls ever make. Never, ever let your friends down. You can tell them how you feel and even make a loose arrangement so

139

that if *he* phones and asks you to go somewhere amazing, you can cancel. However, so many girls find themselves friendless because they give up everything for their new love and when they re-emerge from what turned out to be a very short-lived romance, no-one wants to know them any more.

## Chapter 8

# AND WHERE DID YOU FIND HIM?

### (or What to Do When Your Parents Don't Adore Your Friends)

You are probably pretty familiar with parent-speak when it comes to the subject of your friends.

- "Why do you always have to choose the scruffy ones?"
- "Does she have any table manners?"
- "If you ask me, he's too big for his boots."

- "You are too young to have a boyfriend."
- "What is she wearing?"

To which you probably reply:
- "That's not scruffy, that's the grunge look and it was on the Clothes Show, which shows how little you know, so there."
- "You're a snob."
- "Just because he thinks the Tories are rubbish."
- "No, I am not."
- "Clothes – what do you think?"

All of which is mildly counter-productive to say the least and at worst could lead to one of those arguments in which your father turns purple and coughs up his toasted teacake, your mother bursts into tears and says, "I did my best to bring you up decently and this is how you repay me" and the cat leaves home to live in the bus shelter down the street. It is a fact that your friendships can be a source of friction in the family.

## WHY ARE PARENTS OFTEN CRITICAL OF YOUR FRIENDS?

### 1. *BECAUSE THEY ARE SCARED*

Yes, we are back to that again. They are probably frightened out of their heated rollers by everything from the possibility of your sniffing glue or getting mugged to whether you will forget all the things they taught you about good manners and writing to Aunt Ethel every month and being honest and caring and ... so on.

## 2. *BECAUSE, SOMEWHERE DEEP DOWN, THEY FEEL JUST THE TINIEST BIT JEALOUS OF YOUR FRIENDS*
They have had your adoration and devotion for a decade or so. Now suddenly you are starting sentences with "But Donna says ..." or "Donna does it that way ..." or "William does it better than Dad because ..." They know it is silly and un-grown-up to feel jealous, but that doesn't make the feeling go away.

## 3. *BECAUSE SEEING YOU WITH YOUR FRIENDS MAKES THEM REALISE HOW MUCH TIME HAS PASSED SINCE THEY WERE 14 AND IT MAKES THEM FEEL OLD*
They are not old; they are not even halfway to their sell-by date. But when your mum sees you dressed up for a night out, and then catches sight of her expanding waistline and sagging chin, she feels discarded and dowdy. And when your dad hears your friend Craig talking about how he ran 200 metres in 0.00004 seconds, he feels unfit and saggy too, especially since this morning he ran for a bus and took until lunchtime to recover. So they say things like "Take that make-up off this instant," and "That boy thinks he is God's gift to creation," when what they really mean is, "I wish I was young again."

## 4. *BECAUSE YOUR CODE OF CONDUCT AND THEIRS ARE DIFFERENT*
Parents go for washing in a big way, they love to see boys in ironed shirts and they are rather keen on people who

talk in sentences rather than those monosyllabic "er", "nah", "ya" and "dunno" noises. *You* know that your friend does wash (and then spends two hours trying to make himself look like something from under Waterloo Bridge), *you* know that the creased and crumpled look is in and *you* know that the grunts and mutterings are only an attempt to cover up crippling shyness and embarrassment in the face of your mother's "Now what does your father do, dear?" and "You won't do anything silly now, will you?"

5. *BECAUSE EVERYTHING SEEMS STRANGE*
If you belong to a minority culture living in Britain, you probably feel as much at home here as your parents and grandparents did in Bangladesh or Jamaica or Czechoslovakia. But for them, the cultural, religious and social ideals of their home country are all they have to hang on to. It may be that your Indian father does not approve of your white friends or that your mother is worried because you are not following the old religions as strictly as she would like.

6. *BECAUSE THEY MIGHT BE PREJUDICED* (see page 147)

# CHECKLIST FOR ENSURING THAT PARENTS GO ON DISAPPROVING

1. *NEVER TAKE YOUR FRIENDS HOME*
This has the immediate effect of convincing them that

you have something to hide.

## 2. *WHEN YOU DO TAKE THEM HOME, IGNORE YOUR PARENTS TOTALLY*
Eat them out of house and home, leave without clearing away the dishes and of course, never say thank you or tell them where you are going.

## 3. *CRITICISE*
Start every other sentence with "Why can't you be like Angie's mother?" or "Sandeep's mum never yells at him."

## 4. *LIE A LOT*
Tell them you are going to Sarah's house to do homework together when you are really going to hang around the shopping mall. That should build up trust nicely – and they will blame your friends for being a bad influence.

## 5. *NEGLECT YOUR SCHOOL WORK*
Instead, go out, slam doors and shout when your mother mentions that your grades are slipping and say, "It's only an essay" when your father points out that sitting on the telephone won't get you through GCSEs.

## 6. *DON'T TELL THEM WHAT YOU'RE DOING*
Don't tell them anything about where you are or who you're with. And if you're going to be late, don't phone them. Just let them worry about you instead.

# CHECKLIST FOR PARENTS

– Seven ways to guarantee that your kids won't bring their friends home again. (Leave this book open at this page, somewhere where your parents are bound to see it – beside the loo/near the bottle of Safeways Chardonnay/ on top of the TV remote control.)

1. Say, "Why do you have to hang around with someone who has a ring through their nose? You might as well go down the cattle market – ha! ha!"

2. Say, "I can't think why you want to join the Young Liberals – your dad and I have voted Labour all our lives and anyway, what can someone your age know about politics?"

3. Greet the friend with any of the following: "So you are Megan's little friend?"; "Take your shoes off, dear"; "I hope we can all be mates together"; "You're late"; "You're early"; "What time are you leaving?"

4. Invite your daughter's friend to supper and spend the first half-hour talking about how she still sucks her thumb in bed and can't swim underwater.

5. Bring out the photographs of your son in the nude aged nine months/winning the sack race at playgroup/ picking his nose in the Nativity Play.

6. Use phrases like "I don't know what the world is

coming to"; "You wouldn't get away with that if you were my child"; "When I was young I had to earn what I spent" or "You are not going out looking like that, are you?"

7. Once the friend has left, spend an hour criticising his table manners, speech, shoes, hairstyle and fingernails.

# WHEN PARENTS ARE WRONG

Sometimes your parents will express opinions that you simply cannot handle. You will hear them say things like "Gary has an awful Northern accent. Why can't he speak the Queen's English?"; "I suppose you know that your precious Emma's father is in prison – we don't want you going around with her any more"; "We don't want you to go round to Rajiv's house – those sort of people don't live like us."

## HOW TO GET YOUR PARENTS ON YOUR SIDE

1. *ANSWER THEIR QUESTIONS – EVEN THE SARCASTIC ONES – HONESTLY*
"What do you see in him?"
"He makes me laugh, he is really caring about the environment and we have great talks together."

"Why can't you choose friends from your own race?"
"I like to have a multi-mix of friends – after all, we live in

a multiracial society now, don't we?"

"Why can't you have a friend who dresses nicely?"
"Alice looks great to me, Mum – that's the in look right
now. I expect your Mum disapproved of white boots and
miniskirts in the sixties, didn't she?"

"Why do you have to go around with a jailbird's
daughter?"
"Just because Emma's dad has made a mistake, it doesn't
make Emma bad, Mum. And I reckon she needs her
friends more than ever at a time like this."

## 2. IF THEY BLAME YOUR FRIENDS FOR SOMETHING THAT IS NOT THEIR FAULT, TELL THEM – BUT NICELY
*Father:* "I knew that if you got in with that Sharon, your
grades would drop."
*You:* "It's nothing to do with Sharon, Dad – I am just
finding Maths really tough this term."

*Mother:* "Since you've been going around with Holly, you
don't lift a finger to help in the house. She's a bad
influence."
*You:* "I'm sorry I haven't done much lately – it's just that
we are all working so hard on the school panto and I
forget. I'll do the dishes tonight."

*Father:* "I don't know why you have to imitate the way
Graham speaks. What's wrong with your normal voice –
not good enough for you, are we?"

*You*: "I didn't know I sounded different – I suppose when you are with someone a lot you do pick up the odd speech similarity. Why don't you like it?"

## FRIENDS FROM DIFFERENT CULTURES

When two kids from very different backgrounds become good friends, it can sometimes cause problems with the families. In an ideal and perfect world, everyone would be tolerant, everyone would like everyone else and no-one would have any hang-ups or prejudices. But this is not an ideal world.

When Zara, who is Jewish, started getting friendly with Shamim, who is Iranian and a member of the Baha'i faith, they got on like a house on fire. "We met at an inter-schools pubic speaking competition and started going out together soon after. His parents don't have any problem with my religion – both Judaism and Baha'i are old faiths and we share many of the same moral and ethical values. The thing that Shamim's family can't handle is the fact that I am a female friend. They won't even let me sit down next to him when I visit their house. They ask him things like "Why do you need her when you have the family?" When I visit, I would love to have a chat with his mother and explain things, but she speaks very little English and it would be hard to involve Shamim by asking him to translate."

Zara's parents liked Shamim and accepted the relationship but they were worried by his parents' attitude to their daughter. Shamim thought that some of the problem wass due to the fact that his family believed that nothing should divert his attention from his school work. "In Iran, the work ethic is second only to family in importance. Also I know that it must be me who compromises on a friendship and not my parents. Our faith decrees that if your father gives you poison, you must drink it. It would be unthinkable to go against his word."

After a lot of heartsearching, Shamim and Zara stopped seeing one another. "The problems were too big for us to handle – but maybe one day, when we are both at university, things might be easier."

# Chapter 9

# I'D LIKE TO TEACH THE WORLD TO SING ...

*"Instead of loving your enemies,
treat your friends a little better"*
**(Edgar Watson Howe)**

In a perfect world, we would all be surrounded by loving friends and devoted family who were anxious to smooth our path, mop our brow and generally make our passage through life as trouble-free as possible. But we all know that even in the best-regulated lives, little hiccups occur and there are days when we wake up convinced that nobody loves us, nobody understands and the world might very well end by lunchtime. What we all need on days like these is A STRATEGY!

# STRATEGIES FOR FRIENDLESS DAYS

## 1. PAMPER YOURSELF

Making a fuss of yourself is a great way to begin feeling better. You don't have to spend a fortune – try some of these ideas when the blues hit.

• Try a new wash in/wash out colour on your hair.

• Dig out all those old school photos and all those snapshots taken on school trips and make a collage of your past life. See just how far you have come in a few short years and consider how much further you can go in the next few.

• Write long letters to all your friends who have moved away from town – by the time the next bad day hits you, they will have written back.

• Turn out your wardrobe. Throw out all the old clothes

you never wear, re-vamp any that can be given a second lease of life and try dyeing some of your old T-shirts.

• Exercise is a great way to banish the blues. If you can't find anyone to play sport with, go for a vigorous bike ride, take a run, do 300 backward skips or go swimming.

• "Down" days are *not* the days to diet. Treat yourself to a bar of chocolate, a cream eclair or a bag of lemon sherbets and curl up with a pile of magazines while you indulge.

• Read *Thirteen Something,* which is a brilliant book by Jane Goldman about being a teen. After a couple of chapters, you will realise that the way you feel is quite normal and better still, you will be fired with enthusiasm to do something.

• Do something for someone else. Visit your gran and cook her lunch, offer to help your mum turn out the attic (you never know what goodies may lie hidden there) or clean your dad's car. It may sound like a bind but you store up a lot of Brownie points for yourself and believe it or not, you end up feeling very satisfied at the end of it.

## 2. STOP BEING SO HARD ON YOURSELF

Don't sit there saying "I'm a glob, everyone hates me" or "Why was I born so thick?" Be gentle with yourself. Make a list of all the nice things about you – and believe me, there will be plenty. Understand that everyone is human and maybe the friends who have rejected you are going through funny patches themselves. It isn't necessarily your fault that you are alone today.

## 3. LOOK AHEAD

So today is a bad day. So what do you want to change in your life? Time for another list. Make three headings:

*WHAT I WANT TO ACHIEVE:*
*... THIS WEEK*
*... BY NEXT YEAR*
*... BY THE TIME I'M 21*

Then write them all down. This week you might want to get your hair cut short, finish your maths assignment, pluck up the courage to dive off the top board and see the latest film. By next year, you might want to have made it into the hockey team, persuaded your mum and dad to let you redecorate your bedroom, applied for Sixth Form College and learned how to play squash. And by the time you are 21, you could be at university, or working overseas, or living in a flat in London ... it's up to you. Knowing where you want to go is the first step to getting there.

# WHAT'S CRUCIAL NOW WON'T MATTER NEXT YEAR

If your best friend dumps you or your bosom buddy moves miles away, it can seem like the world as you know it is falling apart. If you don't get invited to Carol Crossthwaite's birthday bash or are left out of the gang's trip to Alton Towers, you feel as if life is never going to go your way. But the great news is that nothing lasts forever. However bad things are now, there will come a time when you don't even remember the things that upset you so much today.

Melanie is 19 and in her first year at university. "I was not a very popular person in the general sense of the word when I was at school. I was moderately clever but really shy and I used to hate crowds of people. I used to copy my schoolfriends' hairstyles and dress in an attempt to get 'in' with them, but I was always on the fringe and I was convinced that I was destined to go through life alone – I never knew what to say to boys, and other girls made me feel silly and inadequate. I have always wanted to be a marine biologist and that is not the sort of thing that people think is very normal! Anyway, things couldn't be more different now. I have made a lot of friends in my college and when I went on a scuba-diving course this summer I met this great guy and we have been going out for four months now. Now I worry much less about what people think – I dress to please me – and Sam, of course! –

and I am beginning to like myself. Life couldn't be better."

Tony's story is rather different. He is now 23 and is on a retail management training scheme with a nationwide chain of supermarkets. "When I look back on my years at secondary school, I cringe. In those days, all that mattered to me was being one of the cool dudes and making an impression. I did the minimum amount of work possible, but yes, I was pretty popular. I was good at sport and had a pretty wicked sense of humour and never minded having a laugh – often at other people's expense. I couldn't resist a dare and was always getting into trouble – although I stopped short of doing anything really stupid or getting suspended or anything like that. My two best mates were Alec and Rob. We did everything together, covered up for one another when there was trouble and were never apart. We thought it would be like that for life. The funny thing is, when we left school, Alec went into the Army and I had one postcard and then heard nothing. Rob did loads of odd jobs for a while and then went off to Spain to work in a bar for the summer. I haven't heard from him since. I left school with only three GCSEs but I retook exams and got in on this training scheme. I've made a lot of friends – but I know that in ten years' time, they may all have moved on. Still, I reckon if I have one really good friend left, I will be lucky. It's not the number you have that matters, but how good they are as mates."

Friends you have at 14 may turn out to be the last people you would choose at 20 – but the reverse can happen.

When Val was at school, she longed to be part of the in set, led by a girl called Jo. "Jo was everything I wanted to be – pretty, clever, witty and very popular with the kids and the teachers alike. But she never had any time for me – she wasn't horrid or anything, she just didn't seem to see me." Six years later, Val was working as a courier for a holiday company on a campsite in France. "A couple of girls came into the office and as I looked up, I actually gasped out loud – one of them was Jo. We got chatting, reminiscing about school and old friends, and we exchanged addresses. When I went back to England at the end of the season, I phoned Jo and we met for lunch. Since then we have met up regularly and next summer we are planning to go to Italy together to work for the same tour company. The friendship I longed for at 14 finally happened – and it was worth waiting for!"

Have you ever looked at those photo quizzes in the Sunday supplements? The ones where they show you a snapshot of a famous celebrity when they were a child and you have to guess who they are? Sometimes the person's facial characteristics as a child are so similar to their present looks that no-one has any trouble recognising. "My goodness," you cry, "he hasn't changed one bit." But of course, he has. Everyone does. Even if, from the outside, the bone structure, the eyes, the smile are the same, you can bet that inside, the person is different. Every day that you are alive you gain new experiences and it is experience that moulds people. You are not the same person now as you were at five years old. Why? Because you have met new people, tried new things, learned new facts, made some mistakes – and learned not to make the same ones again – and had time to think hundreds of thoughts, all of which have combined to make you the person you are today.

It's an exciting thought – just think how much more you will have changed and developed in another five years. Or ten. Or 20. That is what is so exhilarating about life – nothing stays the same. So however bad something may seem now, take heart from the fact that in a year it will seem much less important – and in five years, you may even have forgotten it happened.

Caroline Miller is 44 and has two grown-up sons. "When I was at school, I was not at all popular. I was very fat, shy, and my parents were very strict with me, not letting me have many friends home to play. It was an all-girls school and you know how bitchy young girls can be. I got the nickname Old Fatty Thighs and kids used to laugh when I ran, as I got puffed long before they did. As I got older, the only way I could be 'in' at school was as part of the Drama Club – I was good at acting and never minded playing the 'fat' roles – Sir Toby Belch in *Twelfth Night* for instance. But I grew up thinking I would never have many friends." Caroline married and had two sons and joined a local volunteer group, driving the disabled to the shops. "Then I joined the WRVS and suddenly I had lots of friends, and felt I was doing some good. I organised fundraising events for the local disabled groups and ended up knowing half the town! When the boys were older, I went back to full-time work, running the regional office of a national charity. Since then, I have travelled all over the country on their behalf, lecturing about the organisation and even meeting members of the Government and Royal Family. Not bad for Old Fatty Thighs!"

Which all goes to show that if you are not satisfied with the way things are going now, it can all change. There is only one person who has to want it to – YOU!

## THE PERFECT FRIEND – YOU!

Pam Brown, who wrote a lot of jolly sensible things on the subject of friendship, once said, "Love is blind: friendship quietly closes its eyes." In other words, friends know that you are not perfect and you know that they are not 100 per cent fault-free – and it doesn't matter a jot. Being the perfect friend is not about having a 22-inch waist, coming top in Geography, being loaded down with designer gear or giving lavish birthday presents. It is about being there when your friend's dog has just been run over; it is about understanding that because Rajiv's family don't approve of dancing in public, it doesn't make him a bad person. Friends enjoy the good times together but never run off when the going gets tough. Friends don't say, "Let me know if you need me" and then come up with a dozen things they have to do this minute when you ring because you need them NOW. Friends share their clothes, their thoughts, their library books, their ice pops. But most of all, friends share their time and themselves. To be the perfect friend, you need only be the sort of friend you would like to have. The best thing you can give a friend is yourself.

*Also by Rosie Rushton*

## Staying Cool, Surviving School

The prospect of secondary school can seem terrifying – especially if you've been listening to those exaggerated horror stories told to you by older siblings and friends. But don't despair! Learn the real truth and find out the survival strategies.

# Just Don't Make a Scene, Mum!
The trials and tribulations of five teenagers

## Is there anything more embarrassing than parents?

Not according to these teenagers. From out-of-date parents who dress Jemma like a child or Sumitha's; whose cultural traditions won't allow for a trendy haircut, to  Chelsea's agony-aunt mother who thinks she can still wear mini-skirts and Laura's with her geeky new toy-boy. Meanwhile, Jon's father brags about his son's academic brilliance and wants him to become  a lawyer, when nothing could be further from Jon's mind.

The paths of all these teenagers (and their totally cringe-worthy parents) cross and part throughout this hilarious book.

'. . . cool and diverting comedy . . .'
– *The Times*

'An essential read . . . Belly-achingly funny . . .' – *19*